MEDUSA

Rosie Hewlett

SilverWood

Published in 2021 by SilverWood Books

SilverWood Books Ltd
14 Small Street, Bristol, BS1 1DE, United Kingdom
www.silverwoodbooks.co.uk

ISBN 978-1-80042-066-3 (paperback)
ISBN 978-1-80042-067-0 (ebook)

British Library Cataloguing in Publication Data
A CIP catalogue record for this book is
available from the British Library

Page design and typesetting by SilverWood Books

For my mum and dad,
thank you for everything.

A Note from the Author

Mythology is all about sharing stories and it is human nature to weave our own thread into each story we tell, adding a little piece of ourselves into the narrative. This is what I love most about myths. They are all part of an incredible, vivid canvas that welcomes storytellers to add their own mark, allowing the tales to flourish and grow, to twist and turn, to adapt and evolve. I believe this is why they have endured for so long and why they will continue to live on for generations to come.

When writing *Medusa*, I followed this same tradition of myth, to retell but also reimagine. Therefore, there will be parts of this story that are very familiar and parts that will be entirely new. I hope you enjoy my version and I encourage you all to continue sharing these incredible stories and adding your own, unique mark.

Rosie Hewlett

Voice.

I was beautiful once.

I would not recommend it.

That might come as a surprise to you. A lot of the things I am about to tell you probably will, because there is a lot this world does not know about me. You see, my story has been retold and reimagined so many times over, sometimes even I do not recognise it.

I suppose when you hear my name you think of the usual picture – deadly eyes, a hideous face, that famous crown of snakes. Well, I am sorry to disappoint, but the truth is I was actually fairly ordinary, for a time at least. You see, you really shouldn't believe everything you read. Storytelling can be such a dangerous thing.

I have been called many things in my time:

Seductress.

Liar.

Monster.

Killer.

Rape victim.

People seem to forget that last one.

But history is written by the winners. Or, more simply, history is written by men. People seem to forget that as well. And this is why my story has never really been 'my' story. How could it be, when my voice never had a place in its retelling? I, like so many others, have fallen casualty to the narrative of men. My life has been ground down by their words, forcing me into the stifling confines of a cliché, a prop to bolster their own egos. An endless echo of lies, ringing throughout generations, haunting me.

Even now, in this modern world, my voice has still not been heard. Instead, I have been reduced to something even worse, a label to shame other women with, a brand logo.

Well, I am tired of it.

It is time for me to tell it for myself, in my own words.

Why now, you might ask, after all this time? I suppose, a part of me has been inspired by modern-day voices, those voices that are shaking the very foundations their injustices have been built upon. Yes, we can still hear you down here in the beyond and I like to keep up to date with how the world is ever changing, ever evolving, ever continuing on its quest to destroy itself. You could hear us too, you know, if you bothered to listen back.

Though, I suppose if I am being entirely honest, the main reason I have not spoken out sooner is because I have been afraid. I know that probably seems comical to you. The infamous Medusa *afraid*? But it is the truth. I have been afraid of facing my past and breathing life into those demons I have tried to lay to rest for so long. In telling my story I would risk awakening that darkness inside me once again, that darkness which nearly consumed me.

So, it felt safer to hide within my silence. I had hoped that if I kept quiet then history would simply forget about me. After all, what was I in the grand scheme of things? My 'reign of terror' only lasted a handful of months. There are monsters out there who have inflicted misery for centuries, surely my name would be lost in their destructive wake? How I wished that would be the case. For, if the world moved on and forgot my past, perhaps I could too. Then I would finally be able to rest in peace.

But that never happened, did it? The world did not forget. My story continues to endure, even now in a world so alien from the one I knew. It is one thing to live a tragic life, but it is a whole other kind of torment to witness your life wrongly retold time and time again, clumsily passed from generation to generation. I watch the cracks form with every retelling, unable to stop the lies seeping in and suffocating the truths, twisting me into this silent villain.

I have had enough.

The time has come.

I am Medusa and I am finally going to tell my story. You do not have to believe me, but all I ask is that you listen.

The world owes me that.

Time.

Time was never a friend of mine.

When I was younger I thought I had infinite bounds of it, like handfuls of shimmering ribbon, beautiful and endless. Little did I realise it was always trickling by, the seconds quietly peeling away my innocence, unravelling the safety blanket of youth. In later years, I was forever running out of time. When the world wants your head as a trophy, you know your days are undeniably numbered.

I have often wondered what time feels like when you are old; I never had the gift of experiencing that myself. I imagine it seems endless, but not like it did in youth, rather in a draining and tiresome way. Like being unable to fall asleep when you are so very tired of being awake, you wish the seconds would just slip away.

I guess time is nobody's friend, in the end.

But did you ever wonder whose fault it is?

Chronos. He is the old croak that lets it tick by, endlessly draining the world of its precious seconds. I have never met him, but I hear he is a real kill-joy. In the world of the living, nothing mortal can escape Chronos. His power is like a slow and quiet disease, always fatal in the end. Down here though, he has no influence at all. Minutes, hours, years, centuries – they all swirl around us, like a gentle breeze we are only faintly aware of. It is only when we stop to look up at the living that we realise Chronos' power still endures.

I have never really understood the complexities of how time works. One day, perhaps I will get the chance to ask Chronos. The question that bothers me most is why some memories are lost forever within its folds, whilst others stand out, everlasting?

I remember a lot of my life. And there is a lot I wish I did not. There are memories I wish I could burn from me, like cauterising a wound. Or I would swallow leeches and let them suck this poison from my mind. Whatever it would take, believe me I would do it.

There is a river in the Underworld that would offer me such a release, but the God of Sleep, Hypnos, guards it with ironic vigilance. Only those seeking reincarnation are able to forget and I would rather spend eternity with my demons than face the living realm again.

And yet, I remember all the tiny, sickening details, those little flecks of colour that build up the tapestry of my life. They smother me. Like the smell of salt on his skin, the greyness of her eyes, the bite of the sword as it met my neck.

But, I am getting ahead of myself now and I want to tell my story right. So, I suppose I should be traditional and start at the very beginning.

The Beginning.

I was born amongst the waves.

I can still remember it, even now. The feel of the ocean stirring around me, the water swelling to a point of climax, waves crashing together in a dramatic crescendo, spilling onto land with a great urgency before slowly receding, leaving a gentle bubbling froth clinging to the upturned stones and the formation of a small child – me. This was how I entered the world, my naked body soaked and glistening, gritty with salt.

You see, my parents were the primordial sea Gods, Phorcys and Ceto.

Yes, I have parents. People seem to forget that 'monsters' can have family too.

Our universe began with chaos and it was the primordial Gods who were the first to spring from this void. They brought structure and meaning to the world, laying the very foundations it exists upon to this day. They split the sky from the earth, carved night from day and light from dark. They shaped the seas and raised the mountains, colouring the world with love and life. Amongst these Gods were my parents, who took responsibility for enriching the seas with hidden dangers. Of course, Chronos was there too, shackling the world to the seconds he lets slip by so freely.

Many of these early Gods have been forgotten now. I still find it amazing how so many powerful beings have been overlooked by history and yet my story endures. *Why me?* I so often wonder.

I never really knew my parents. I have never even met Phorcys, my father. They did not want much to do with me. I was born an ordinary mortal and was therefore, in their eyes, a disappointment.

I see you raising your eyebrows. *Medusa? An ordinary baby?*

This is one of the many things about me on which history disagrees. Centuries of men posturing across pages of baseless claims, disagreeing for the sole purpose of feeding their plump egos. Well, I can confirm for the record, I was born a normal human child. In general, I find that most monsters are made, not born. Perhaps you should remember that next time you encounter one.

"What is this?" Stheno asked when she found our mother cradling my tiny body to her breast. She was one of the oldest of my mother's children. Her name meant 'forceful' and she certainly lived up to it.

"Your sister." My mother's voice rippled like the waves. My sisters had told me she had been calm, for someone who had just ripped themselves apart to create life.

"Why is she so...normal?" Euryale, my other sister, sneered from behind. "She's basically a mortal."

"She *is* a mortal," my mother responded, her voice suddenly sharp.

My sisters had stared incredulously at me. I was so normal, so ordinary, so...disappointing. How could I be related to the likes of them?

"Well, I am not caring for any *human*." Stheno waved her hand dismissively, heading off up the beach with defiant steps. Suddenly, a wave rushed in and scooped Stheno off her feet, forcing her to crash down onto the stony floor. "Mother!" She let out a furious shriek, as the waves sucked backwards over the pebbles, bubbling with wicked laughter.

"Do you think I would degrade myself to raise a mortal child?" My mother's voice was firmer now, her dark eyes narrowed. "Here, you will take her." Euryale reached out, taking my plump body in her awkward embrace.

"But what are we supposed to do with her?" Her voice hovered on the edge of a tantrum.

"Whatever you want. It is no child of mine." Euryale opened her mouth to protest, but before she could our mother had already slipped off into the ocean, her scaly skin melting beneath its restless surface.

"Now what?" Euryale and Stheno shared a long look and then stared down at the tiny child before them – their new baby sister.

"Well I don't want her."

"Well neither do I!"

"You're the one holding her."

"That's not fair!"

"Finders keepers."

After a quick and heated debate, they decided the best decision was to leave me with my own kind. Mortals.

There was a temple nearby where a lonely priestess served. My sisters were not overly familiar with mortal behaviour, but they assumed a solitary woman would accept an abandoned child – surely it would be in her human nature?

They had heard of this temple many years before, when it had become entangled in the latest gossip spread across everyone's eager lips. Despite its reputation, it was not until later years that I learnt the truth about the temple's tragic history and how the surrounding land came to be known as cursed.

This temple had once overlooked a proud yet modest city. As time passed, this city began to flourish and drew the attention of Poseidon, who saw his own greatness reflected within its success. He assumed himself the patron God of the city and began to tell this to all who would listen.

"Brother, if you are their patron God then why have they built a temple in honour of Athena?" Zeus asked him one day with a poorly disguised smirk.

I'm sure you can imagine Poseidon's furious shock when he discovered the people had chosen to honour Athena over him. Unable to face this rejection, Poseidon decided that if the people desired the Goddess of War so badly, then he would bring war to them. He destroyed the city, reducing it to rubble and dust, for if he could not have it, then nobody could. The temple was all that was left standing, for Poseidon knew he could not offend Athena by destroying her sanctuary. That would undeniably be a step too far against Zeus' favourite daughter.

Some claim the few survivors tried to rebuild the city, but they soon fell victim to a depraved tribe of centaurs. Though Athena's temple endured, the land would forever remain deserted, for it came to be believed that any who dwelled there would meet a violent end. Perhaps there is some truth in that, if my life is anything to go by. Though I do not like to entertain the shallowness of hearsay. Rumours are a terrible thing, are they not? Like a disease passing from person to person, mutating into all kinds of hideous things.

I should tell you now, before you waste any of your time, there is no surviving record of that temple. Athena made sure of that. She obliterated all evidence from the Earth when she discovered that I had…well, I will get to that part later.

Anyway, where was I? Oh yes. The solitary priestess. She had been the only one to stay after the devastation, the only one who would not abandon her Goddess. Loyal and lonely, my sisters thought she would be a suitable mortal for their baby sister. And so, they left me on those temple steps and that is how I came to be abandoned twice in the first few hours of my life.

Of course, I do not really remember any of this myself. I was filled in by my sisters in later years. They liked to cackle over how indifferent my mother had been, exaggerating all the plans they had had to get rid of me.

"We considered feeding you to wolves…"

"Or sacrificing you to Hades…"

"Or throwing you off a cliff to see if you'd sprout wings like us…"

"Or tossing you into the sea to see if mother would change her mind…"

Needless to say, they had dark senses of humour.

I do not judge my mother for abandoning me. History will remember her as the Mother of Monsters, she bore fearsome, infamous children. She couldn't have the likes of me ruin her track record, could she?

And besides, I cannot complain, because I had a happy childhood and that is more than most can say.

Childhood.

My childhood memories are like faded dreams encased in lingering sensations. The sweet smell of incense, the cool touch of marble, the choking smoke after a sacrifice and the shock of cold water purifying my skin each morning. These memories all glow inside me like soft embers refusing to die away; if I focus hard enough I imagine I can feel their gentle warmth. It's comforting, to remind myself I had once been happy. Though, if I try to reach out too far or hold on too tightly, these memories turn cold and bitter, tainted by the darker corners of my mind.

The priestess found me shortly after my sisters left.

As they had predicted, the priestess welcomed me into her life without hesitation. She had spent years praying for a companion and believed the Gods had finally answered her. As if the Gods would ever be that generous.

I never knew her real name; she used to say she did not have one anymore. She just had me call her *Theia*, Auntie. I do not know what horrors Theia witnessed when her city was destroyed, or why she was the only one to stay. In fact, now I think on it, I knew very little at all about Theia's past. I suppose when you are a child you do not think to ask about before, all you ever focus on is the now. I wish I still lived like that.

It was Theia who gave me my name, Medusa. I am aware my

17

name is now synonymous with monsters, but it might surprise you to know it actually means 'protector'. Theia had wanted me to protect her temple and so named me as such. Irony has a cruel sense of humour, does it not? But, I guess you just have to laugh, or else you will go mad.

Or maybe I already am.

I was raised in the temple by Theia and I was taught from my earliest years to live piously. I dedicated myself and my life to Athena, spending every day serving her. It seemed like an honourable duty, back then. The fact that Athena's temple was all that remained of the lost city made our responsibility feel even more important. We had to protect it at all costs.

I suppose it might seem an odd backdrop for a childhood, a solitary temple set against the bones of a city, but how was I to know any different? I would play for hours amongst the rubble and debris, oblivious to the dark reality lying beneath the ruins. Ignorance is such a fragile gift.

I often wonder what would have happened if I had been left outside a different temple, had dedicated my life to another God. Perhaps then my life would not have spiralled so drastically out of control. Take Hestia for example, the Goddess of the Hearth. I cannot imagine her punishing her priestesses like Athena did – she seems too warm, too welcoming. But then again, you really cannot trust any of the Gods, that much I know for sure. The safest life for a mortal is one free of divine interference. Sadly, I was never granted that luxury.

Theia was a thin wisp of a woman; her body was all angles, her features lost years ago between the creases of ancient wrinkles. I cannot imagine what Theia would have looked like in her youth. To me, she was just one of those people who are perpetually old. She was a difficult person to read. Strict, but never unkind.

Though her affection was stiff and awkward, like wearing clothes that did not quite fit. Perhaps it is because she had been alone for so long and had never been around children. But she did her best and I did not know any better – so it worked for us.

Priestess life was simple enough, considering our temple was so remote. I was mostly in charge of cleaning and tidying. My most precious duty was dusting the cult statue of Athena each morning and evening and I can still remember the rush of excitement the first time Theia gifted me with this task.

"This is an incredibly important duty, Medusa." Theia always spoke with such weight to her words, she was never one for small talk. "This statue is the physical embodiment of our Wise Goddess and therefore we must treat it as if it were Athena herself standing before us. To neglect this statue would be to offend our Great Goddess." As Theia spoke, I remember looking up at the marble figure looming over me, feeling my chest swell with adoration. Athena was carved in her glorious battle gear, holding a shield in one hand and spear in the other. Her expression was one of calm collectedness, her lips set in neither a frown nor a smile. As I gazed into Athena's blank eyes, I imagined the Goddess turning to look down at me, giving a reassuring nod of her head: *You can do this, Medusa.*

Needless to say, I took my duties extremely seriously. Each time I cleaned that statue I treated it as if it were a mini ceremony within itself, one that had to be executed to absolute perfection, in order to please the Goddess. Everything I did back then was to please her.

It is hard to think about now, but in those days I utterly adored Athena. She was my idol, but more than that, I even naïvely considered her my friend. Growing up alone, living with a woman of few words, I found myself talking endlessly to that statue. I would tell her everything and anything. I would gush about how much I admired her, confide in her about my most private thoughts… I would blab on and on, as if I actually thought she was somewhere listening. As if she actually cared.

I often imagined the warm touch of her hand on my shoulder; I could visualise so clearly how firm and reassuring it would feel. At times I even swore I felt her presence radiating through the cool marble, prickling over my skin, as if Athena were trying to tell me: *I am here, I am listening.*

But of course, these were just the wishful thoughts of a lonely child. Athena did not listen nor care. She never had and never would.

However, despite my loneliness, I was content. You know, I have been thinking about it and I have come to realise that contentment is something you only ever truly appreciate in hindsight. That is why I find there is always something slightly melancholic about it, but perhaps that is just me.

The days were long and quiet, the months yawning out and melting into one another. Peaceful. I do not remember ever feeling bored, perhaps because I did not know any other way of life. Of course, I was often lonely, but that was just something I learnt to live with. We did occasionally get visitors, weary travellers seeking shelter and guidance from Athena. But Theia would always shoo me away when this happened, keeping me busy with some out-of-sight task.

Sometimes, we would make the long trek to the nearest town to stock up on provisions. It was a day's round trip – we would always set off before the sun God, Helios, had even started his own daily journey and we would not get home until well after his chariot had melted beyond the horizon.

I was always excited about these excursions, I was fascinated by the bustle and hubbub of city life. I can still visualise the first time Theia let me accompany her. I must have been only eight or nine summers old and I had been utterly engrossed in this other world, bursting with so many new sights and sounds and smells, every corner brimming with life – it felt so alien from my own quiet existence. I can remember feeling the excitement and wonder swell inside me, slightly tinged by that tug of innate unease towards the unknown.

During that initial visit I came across a small clump of boys. It was the first time I had ever seen children my own age. They were wrestling one another, their faces grubby and glowing with carefree joy. I had been so engrossed in watching them, I had not noticed Theia walk off ahead.

"Who are you?" one boy asked loudly, when he caught me looking.

"Girls aren't supposed to be out on their own," another said, his words slightly whistling from his missing front teeth.

"My name is Medusa." I offered them a smile and to my delight, they returned it.

"You're not from round here," one boy observed, his tone sharp.

"I serve at Athena's temple." I felt my smile faltering.

"There ain't no temple to Athena round here."

"There is… Northward, by the ocean." They gave a collective gasp, their sudden realisation causing the atmosphere to grow tense.

"You're from the cursed city!" one of them whispered nervously.

"Cursed?" This was the first I had ever heard of these rumours.

"Don't you know what happened?" a slightly shyer boy asked from the back, his freckly face only just visible over his friends' shoulders.

"Poseidon did it," one blurted eagerly. "He killed everyone! Stabbed them with his trident!" He began to make excitable swooping motions, gripping an invisible weapon.

Before I had a chance to respond, I felt a cold grip close around my wrist, wrenching me backwards. I swung round and was met with Theia's stern, pointed face.

"What are you doing, Medusa?" she snapped.

"I was just talking-"

"Listen here, child. We are priestesses to Athena and we are always representing her, wherever we go. Therefore, we must present ourselves accordingly." She kept her bony fingers laced round my wrist, squeezing tighter to emphasise her words. "Never forget that." I remember glancing backwards to see the children all watching with curious eyes, whispering to one another behind cupped hands. I lowered my head and followed after Theia, mimicking her measured steps, whilst silently wondering if a God could really be capable of such a monstrous act.

How innocent I was.

That evening, as we trudged our way back to the temple, picking our way through the dusty bones of the destroyed city, I kept hearing the boy's words echo in my mind: *the cursed city.* I had never feared the rubble of the city before, but suddenly I felt a new kind of anxiety lodging inside me. I remember the darkness had been closing in, collecting around the debris and distorting it into monstrous shapes, feeding my newfound fear. Everywhere I looked shadows crouched in corners, like creatures waiting to strike. *Cursed.*

When we finally reached the temple I realised I was shivering. I tried to steady my hands as I scooped up the ceremonial water, watching the moonlight catch in each fallen droplet as I cleansed my skin.

"What is wrong, child?" Theia eyed me closely. I was ready to mask my jitteriness with a simple lie, but something made me hesitate. Perhaps it was curiosity, or perhaps it was being unable to lie under Athena's marble glare. Either way, I decided to speak the truth.

"The boys in the town… They said this land is cursed." I studied Theia's creased face, trying to decipher her reaction. A slight frown had gathered at the corner of her lips, but her eyes remained guarded. She never gave anything away easily.

"Is that so?" She nodded slowly, indicating for me to step aside so she could purify herself.

"Why would they say such a thing?" I prompted, as she dipped her thin hands into the water.

"People say a lot of things," she replied evasively. Perhaps I should have sensed Theia did not want to pursue this conversation, but being young and stubborn, I decided to press on.

"But is it true?"

"Medusa." Theia turned to me, her voice suddenly sharp. The moonlight caught in her eyes, causing them to appear paler than usual, eerie. "We are priestesses to Athena. Participating in gossip is entirely beneath us."

"But what did happen…to the city?" Theia had turned away from me now as she headed further inside. "They said Poseidon did it… Is that true? Could a God do such a thing?"

"It is not a story for today."

"That's what you always say." My voice wavered close to a whine.

"It was destroyed. That is what happened. What else is there to know?" Theia snapped coldly. I opened my mouth to speak, but she continued. "By Athena's divine protection the temple survived and it is our duty to ensure the temple continues to endure. We must do everything in our power, do you understand, Medusa? This is all that is left. We must protect it at all costs." I was shocked to see her eyes were wet and sparkling now. I had never seen Theia cry before. "Do you understand? Do you?" She gripped my arms, her hands trembling.

"Yes. I understand," I replied, unnerved by her sudden intensity. "I promise I will protect the temple, Theia. I promise."

Sisters.

For the longest time I did not know where I came from. All I remembered were the waves. Our temple overlooked the ocean and every morning I would walk out along the cliffs and feel a deep aching inside me, a longing to be back within the water.

I never long for the ocean anymore.

Sometimes I wondered whether I had been in a shipwreck and if perhaps the rest of my family had been lost at sea. Or what if they had survived and were somewhere out there looking for me? Occasionally, I even considered whether Theia was right and I really *was* a gift from Athena and if so, did that mean I had some higher purpose? But how could I ever achieve it if I did not know what it was? Or what if I was just an abandoned baby after all? Why had my mother not wanted me? Was there something wrong with me?

When I was eleven summers old I finally found my answers. Or rather, they found me.

"Hello, stranger."

The day had started like any other. I was on my usual morning walk when I heard that voice cut across the salty breeze. I was so used to the silence that blanketed my life, it made me jump out of my skin. I turned, but nobody was there. I was only met with the familiar sight of the ocean yawning out before me. Helios was just setting off into the sky, his morning light shattering across the water's restless surface.

I thought I must have imagined it, so I carried on walking.

"Aren't you going to say 'hi' back?" Another playful voice. I reeled round again, quicker this time, eyes alert.

"Who's there?" I grabbed a nearby stick, holding it up like a mighty sword. I could hear their laughter crackling in the wind.

"That's no way to greet family…" Suddenly, I felt an upwards force on my arms and before I knew it my feet had left the ground. I let out a scream, but it immediately got caught in the rushing wind surrounding me. I tried to look up but the sun was blinding, causing inky spots to bloom across my vision. When I had finally blinked them away I realised the ground had shrunk far away beneath me. I felt a surge of nausea churn in my stomach.

"LET ME GO!" I writhed against the ironclad grip around my arms.

"If you insist!" the voice chuckled. Suddenly, I was falling through the sky like a stone. I think I screamed, but to be honest I do not really know, it was all a terrifying blur. Right before I hit the ground I felt another jolt in my arms and suddenly I was being gently lowered until my feet delicately touched the stones. The perpetrators finally let go and I immediately keeled over, retching. The ground felt shaky beneath my feet, the world tilting precariously around me.

This was how I met my sisters.

"Not used to flying are we?" They broke into peals of laughter. When the ground finally felt steady again, I managed to look up. Two young women stood before me. They were beautiful.

Yes, my sisters were also born beautiful, this is yet another misconception about us.

"What's that face for? Don't you know who we are?" The one on the left cocked a playful eyebrow, waiting for me to respond, yet all I could do was stare. They were practically identical to one another, with big, dark curls and eyes the colour of a restless sea, similar to my own. But what caught my attention most was their wings, stunningly outstretched behind them, their dark feathers glinting dramatically in the sunlight. I had never seen anything so magnificent in my life. I thought perhaps they might have been Goddesses, so I fell to my knees immediately.

"Oh, get up you silly thing," they cackled, "we are your sisters!"

"Sisters?" I looked up incredulously. They both had that peculiar ageless look about them that all immortals possess.

"Don't you remember? Mortals have such terrible memories, don't they Stheno?"

And so, they told me all about our parents being fearsome Gods of the sea, about my birth and my mother's indifference. They had told me that I was born on the current of a gentle wave and that is why I was soft and delicate – a mortal human. They had been born in the midst of a storm, the waves ripping and crashing around them, crushing their bodies, tearing at their skin. That is why they were strong and powerful – immortals. I am not sure about the validity of these claims, but back then I ate up their every word.

As I listened, I felt a thrill sing through my body. I was related to the *Gods*. It made me feel special, powerful even… Though, as I listened, I remember feeling that excitement quickly begin to shrivel up, as the realisation hardened inside me, cold and heavy, like a stone in the pit of my stomach.

I was a disappointment to my family.

I had been abandoned.

I was unwanted.

*

Why did my sisters come and find me after eleven years of silence? I have sometimes wondered this myself. I did ask them once, but they only replied with indifferent shrugs: "We were bored." I had believed this answer, like I believed everything they told me back then. But now I have had an endless time to reflect, I have come to believe my sisters had been hiding the real reason from me.

You see, I was not the only disappointment within our family. Though Euryale and Stheno were winged immortals, they still paled in comparison to our parents' other children. Our siblings were infamous monsters of the sea, deadly, fearsome creatures who forced Euryale and Stheno to live in their monstrous shadows. My sisters grew up knowing they would never be enough and I think one day they decided they were fed up of being deemed the inadequate daughters. So, they decided to seek out the one sibling they knew would never reject them, the one sibling who would look up to and admire them. In short, I was the ego boost they had sorely needed.

After that day, my sisters visited often. They never stepped foot in the temple and they instructed I say nothing to Theia. They thought she would cast me out if she knew I was born from monsters. I felt an unfamiliar mixture of guilt and excitement at having my first ever secret to keep. We even had our own secret system – my sisters would leave a little pile of rocks outside the temple to indicate they were nearby. It was easy enough for me to find time to slip away. Theia gifted me with a great amount of independence, so long as I made sure my chores were done at the end of each day.

As soon as I spied those rocks, I would hurry out of the temple, my mind buzzing with the excitement of spending another day with my sisters, my *family*. But that eagerness soon faded into something else entirely.

The problem was that my sisters' idea of entertainment was finding impossible challenges for me and proceeding to watch with judging eyes and barely hidden smirks as I failed each time.

"You see that tree over there, Medusa? I'll race you to it."

"You see that island in the distance? Let's go swim out to it."

"You see that wild stag? Go hunt it for us."

At first, I was thrilled just to have the gift of their attention, but as time passed I began to grow hot with frustration as I failed the tasks they could complete so effortlessly. The delight of having sisters gradually soured into envy and even as I grew older and stronger, I was still forever failing to keep up with Stheno and Euryale.

"You see that apple up there? Go get it for me," Stheno ordered one day. Her tone had been casual, as if it were just a simple request, but I can still remember feeling my stomach drop as I turned to look up. The tree was enormous, its knotted branches looming high above our heads, like gnarled limbs reaching upwards towards the sky. Nestled near the top, barely even visible from way down on the ground, a lonely apple was balanced precariously. I was certain my sisters had placed it there on purpose and they could have easily flown up themselves to fetch it, but I did not want to give them the satisfaction of giving up. Just once I wanted to prove them wrong and wipe those smug looks from their faces. I wanted to show them that I was enough.

"Fine," I shrugged, jutting my chin out confidently as I strode towards the trunk of the tree. Euryale and Stheno shared a knowing grin, flopping down on the grass ready to watch another of my vain attempts.

I swallowed as I pressed my hand against the rough bark, steeling myself. *I can do this. I can.* I could hear Euryale and Stheno's stifled giggles as I tried to jump to reach the nearest branch, but my attempts were embarrassingly futile. Stheno muttered something to Euryale and she let out a snort of laughter. I forced myself to ignore them, as I proceeded to place my foot on a bulging knot near the base of the trunk, using it to leverage myself up. Once I had gained purchase on the lowest branch, I carefully hoisted myself upwards, feeling my muscles spasm in protest. After an awkward few moments of trying to heave my body up and over, I finally managed to position myself atop the lowest branch, triumphantly wiping the sweat from my forehead.

"Everything okay, little sister?" Euryale called out, her tone flecked with sarcasm.

I decided to ignore her, focusing instead on finding my footing as I carefully stretched towards the next closest branch, which was thankfully within reach. After a while I found a rhythm as I worked my way cautiously towards the apple. Whilst I clambered closer my mind began to jump ahead, already envisioning my success – the triumphant feel of the waxy apple in my grasp, my sisters' look of surprise as I casually tossed my prize to them, that feeling of victory, so sweet I could almost taste it...

Suddenly, my foot slipped. I scrambled helplessly, my clumsy hands fighting to keep hold of the closest branch, but it was too late. A horrible wave of dread surged through my stomach as I realised what was about to happen. As I fell, I remember the feeling of the branches grabbing and scratching at my body, pulling at my hair. Within seconds, I had landed heavily on the ground, feeling a sharp pain slice up through my legs. I stayed very still for a few moments, waiting for the inevitable onslaught of mockery.

"How about another go, Medusa?" Euryale suggested, barely containing her laughter. I remained still, hoping if I squeezed myself tight enough I would just disappear completely.

"What's wrong, Medusa? Giving up so easily?" Stheno asked, arranging her face in a look of fake innocence.

"I CAN'T DO IT!" I exploded, staggering to my feet.

"Why so, Medusa?" Stheno's voice curled mockingly at the edges. I balled my hands into fists at my side, feeling my palms sting from the fresh wounds. Stheno and Euryale never got cuts or bruises.

"You are so cruel, Stheno," I hissed back at her, rubbing my eyes furiously as I felt the tears begin to spill. *Don't cry, don't cry.*

"Are you going to cry like a baby as well?" She rolled her eyes, lolling her head to one side as if I bored her.

"If you want to give up, then fine, just give up." Euryale shrugged, as she picked up a fistful of wild flowers and began to absentmindedly rip off a petal at a time. "Mortals are so predictable."

"It's not my fault I'm a mortal! I didn't ask for this!" I felt a tantrum bubbling in my throat. "It's not *fair*!"

"Life's not fair, Medusa," Stheno countered coolly, "get over it."

"I hate you both! I wish you never found me! I wish you would just leave me alone forever!" I cried out, before turning to run as far away as my clumsy mortal legs could carry me.

No wonder my mother doesn't want me. My thoughts taunted me hatefully as I ran until my lungs burnt and my legs crumpled beneath me. I finally collapsed by the shore, gulping for air between shuddering sobs. *Useless, useless, useless.* Gradually, my bawling subsided to sniffling hiccups, as I stared out across the ocean. My spiteful thoughts died away, leaving one question running circles in my mind: *why me?* Why was I the one cursed to be so feeble and pathetic, why did I have to be born a disappointment, what had I done to deserve this?

Even now, after all this time, I can still remember how wretched I felt. Perhaps you will think me whiny, but it is important to remember I was just a child back then. I was at that tender age where your problems feel all-consuming, far bigger and more important than the world around you. We have all been there, have we not?

After a while, I did something I had tried countless times before when needing comfort. I called out to Athena. "Please, if you are there, Athena… I could really do with your guidance, wise Goddess."

She did not answer. She never did.

As the lonely silence yawned out before me, I decided to attempt something I had never done before. I tried to summon my mother.

"Mother." My voice was just a breath, as if I was afraid someone might actually hear, though of course I was entirely alone as usual. Then I tried a little louder, "Mother I'm here. Please talk to me." The waves rushed to meet me, bubbling up and kissing my toes, before drawing away again. Was that a sign? I did not know. I never will. "Mother, please." My voice sounded ragged from a sudden rush of overwhelming desperation. I felt the tears begin to spill again. "I want to meet you…please. I'm sorry… I'm sorry I'm a mortal. I'm sorry I have disappointed you. Please, just give me a chance…"

I waited.

And waited.

I do not know how long for. To be honest, I do not know if I ever really believed she would come. And what would I say to her even if she did? She would have no interest in the tears of a mortal child. She was a powerful, fearsome Goddess; why should she care about my dull little life?

I sat staring at the ocean for what felt like hours, until the tears had dried, causing my cheeks to feel stiff and my eyes raw. I felt weighed down by that particular kind of exhaustion you feel after a long cry.

Finally, I was broken from my trance-like state by the sound of my name, "Medusa!" I turned to see Theia's pointy frame hobbling along the shore. I remember thinking I should get up to meet her and yet I remained motionless. I felt oddly numb, as if I were frozen in place. "Medusa, what have you been doing?" She gasped for air when she finally reached me, her face looking even thinner than usual. "I have been looking everywhere for you." Theia sounded like she was about to scold me, but when she registered my expression something in her eyes shifted and eventually softened. "What is wrong, my child?"

"Why was I abandoned?" My voice sounded very small and was lost immediately by a rush of waves. I heard Theia sigh, as she awkwardly lowered herself down beside me, her bones creaking in protest.

"Medusa," she said my name softly, like a promise. When I turned to look at her, she was gazing out across the ocean. "Sometimes things happen in life that seem unfair and often we do not understand why. But you must remember that the Fates always have a plan for us. Every life has been carefully thought and planned out. It might not make sense to you now, but you should take comfort in knowing your life is on the course it was always meant to be on." She rested a delicate hand on my shoulder, it was as close to embracing as we ever got.

"But what if I do not want to be on this course?" I sniffed.

"Unfortunately, my child, we do not have the power to change that." Her dewy eyes found mine and crinkled into a smile. "Not even the Gods can change the Fates. Granted they can blow events off course, but ultimately what will be will always be." The weight of her words hung in the silence that followed, the only sound I could hear was the waves periodically hushing the world around us. It felt like hours passed, or perhaps it was only minutes. Like I said, time is a funny thing.

"Are the Fates good people?" I finally voiced the thought that had been nagging inside me. Theia regarded me slowly for a moment, her face gathered in thought.

"They are Goddesses, Medusa. It is not our place to question them." I nodded as she spoke, deciding not to point out that she had not really answered my question at all. "Now, I think the Fates are wanting you to go home and get some dinner ready," she added with an affectionate nudge of her elbow.

Instead of being comforted by Theia's words, I felt disturbed by the idea of my entire life being decided by beings I had never met. To be honest, it still bothers me now, to think how much power those three crones held in their wrinkled old hands, power that even the King of the Gods himself could not undo.

That night, I woke to find the Fates sitting in the corner of my room, gathered round a spindle and cackling loudly. I saw Clotho, the spinner, weaving the delicate thread of my life, with a sinister smile curled at her lips. Lachesis, the allotter, took my thread in her hands, sniggering as she mulled over what kind of anguish and misery to lace within it.

"Some heartbreak maybe?" Clotho suggested.

"Perhaps a little disease or destruction?" Lachesis grinned.

"Don't forget a healthy dose of misery!" Clotho added.

"And death! Lots of death!" That was Atropos, who would snip the thread and seal the moment your life would end. She held out her rusty shears, licking her dry lips, eagerly waiting to snip, snip, snip...

"NO!" I cried out, jolting myself awake, my entire body gripped in a cold sweat.

This nightmare continued to haunt my dreams each night and during the daytime, my mind would be weighed down by endless questions: would the Fates be kind to me? Or fair at least? I was a good, pious person, so would they not reward me for that? Surely they would treat a priestess fairly? But what if they made a mistake?

I was plagued by these thoughts for months, until one day I had a realisation. I suppose you could call it an epiphany, of sorts. I was busy tidying in the temple, when my attention was caught by a ray of sunlight spilling in from the doorway. This sliver of light was filled with tiny dust motes, dancing lazily within its delicate warmth. I was transfixed, staring at these specks, thinking how small and inconsequential they were to the rest of the world. And that is when it dawned on me. We were all just as insignificant to the glorious Gods. What did I matter to the Fates? Who was I to question these Goddesses' divine bidding? I was of no importance, I was a nobody, a tiny dust mote dancing in their light. Perhaps it sounds strange to you, but this anonymity felt immensely comforting and it was in that moment I made a decision. I decided to trust the Fates, as I blindly trusted all the Gods back then. They were Goddesses, so whatever life they wove for me, it would surely be the right one...

Like I said, I was deeply naïve back then.

And by the way, Fates, if you are listening – Clotho, Lachesis and Atropos – I just wanted to say: screw you.

Sex.

Thankfully, my sisters did not take my tantrum to heart. In fact, they praised me for showing a little fight and even began to ease up on their taunting challenges. Families are a funny thing, aren't they?

As time passed, my sisters and I settled into a more comfortable dynamic. Though I would obviously always be the runt of the family, Euryale and Stheno started to make a notable effort to make me feel more accepted – they would compliment me more and listen to my problems, constantly eager to give me advice (though it was not always the best). However, they still enjoyed winding me up on occasion, as I suppose all big sisters do.

"Medusa, do you know what sex is?" Stheno asked me one day. It was a hazy summer afternoon, the heat hung heavy in the air, too close for comfort. We were lounging in the grass near the temple. I think my hair had been damp and clumpy from having just swum in the ocean, I can still imagine the smell of the salt entangled in my curls. I had felt happy, until Stheno ruined it with that question.

"Well, Medusa?" Her eyes were always piercing, like a predator narrowing in on its prey.

I felt my cheeks immediately grow hot with embarrassment. Theia had taught me a little about sex, or as she called it 'the binding of flesh' (which made it sound eerily violent to me).

But she would only mention it in order to remind me that, as priestesses, we were banned from such activities. We were to be forever virginal, like the great Goddess Athena herself.

Stheno and Euryale talked about sex often. They would gossip endlessly about it in front of me, but whenever I asked questions they would just cackle and say, "We'll tell you when you're older." They loved using that phrase and the authority it gave them. They would often play games like 'which Olympian would you have?' Stheno always said Hades, God of Death, because she liked his "dark broodiness". Euryale, on the other hand, would always pick Dionysus, exclaiming loudly, "He's the *God* of sex! Need I say more?" I would remain silent during these games, knowing full well the response I would get if I tried to join in, "You can play when you're older".

When I did not immediately respond, Stheno continued, "Come on, you're nearly old enough now, aren't you? So you must know *something*."

"She's a priestess," Euryale interjected, her tone derisively posh, "they do not partake in such debauched activities."

"As if!" Stheno cackled. "That old hag has definitely had it."

"Don't talk about Theia like that." My voice wavered slightly, as Stheno flashed me a challenging look. I added hurriedly, "And you are right, Euryale, I dedicated myself to Athena. So I will be a virgin forever."

"That's a real tragedy!" Stheno gasped dramatically. "Your life will be so *boring*."

"Won't you miss it?" Euryale frowned, as she absentmindedly made a little pile of beheaded flowers.

"How can I miss what I don't know?" I shrugged, setting my gaze firmly on the ground in front of me and praying the conversation would move on soon.

"Don't you get any *urges?*" Stheno gave me a look, a wicked smile playing at her lips.

"Not really." I glanced away, feeling increasingly uneasy under their scrutiny.

"To be fair, there's not much to entice you round here." Euryale gestured to the empty hillside.

"None of the visitors?" Stheno pressed on. She was like a dog with a bone.

"Yeah, anyone handsome?" Euryale chimed in excitably. I assumed their gossip pools must have dried up, if they were trying to squeeze something juicy from me. Or maybe they just enjoyed watching me squirm.

"No." I shook my head, feeling my cheeks burn violently.

"That's okay, I'm sure someone will come along soon." Euryale grinned at me, giving me an encouraging pat on the leg. "You just have to keep an eye out."

"We could find some men for you, Medusa." Stheno was on her feet, I could already see her mind working, racing five steps ahead of us.

"No, no. I'm not interested." It felt as if I were slowly being cornered. I could feel my chest beginning to tighten. "I have promised myself to Athena."

"Oh please, don't be so boring." Stheno rolled her eyes dismissively. "We'll find you some nice suitors you can have fun with...and we will tell you what to expect and what you can do to make it a little better for yourself..."

"I said NO!" My voice cut across Stheno with uncharacteristic force. My sisters fell silent, regarding me slowly. Euryale looked mildly impressed, Stheno's expression was unreadable, but I think I saw a flicker of irritated disappointment.

"Suit yourself." She shrugged, as if she never really cared in the first place. "If that's really what you want."

"It is," I responded evenly.

We settled into a tense silence, each gazing off in different directions, pretending to be distracted by the view. Suddenly, the warm afternoon felt unbearably hot, I could feel it clinging to my skin, as the sweat slipped down my spine. I shifted uncomfortably, keeping my eyes set firmly away from my sisters.

Finally, to my relief, Euryale broke the heavy tension by saying, "It's not really all it's cracked up to be anyway."

"That's because you always pick the ugliest guys!" Stheno began to howl with laughter and soon they descended into a playful argument, which I could not help but laugh along with.

To be honest, I cannot remember what my feelings were towards sex back then. It is hard to think about, now my view has been so irrevocably damaged. I suppose I must have had certain thoughts or unfamiliar urges, but I would never have dwelled on them, because that would have felt like a betrayal to Athena. Admittedly, I had longed to be a mother one day, but I buried that desire deep inside me, because it just was not possible. I was a virgin priestess; I had to accept these things were never going to be part of my life.

Or so I had thought.

Beauty.

I have heard versions of my story that claim I was transformed into a monster because I gloated too much about being beautiful. Excuse me while I take a moment to laugh. Pah! If only my crimes were that quaint. And besides, what kind of 'crime' is that anyway? A man can sing endlessly of a woman's beauty, but if she acknowledges it herself she is immediately the villain? One day I think I might strain my eyes from rolling them so much.

Anyway, I never cared about being beautiful. I never even liked it. If I had the option to be beautiful again, I would not take it. Let me tell you, being feared was far more fun than being desired.

You might think beauty is a trivial thing to complain about. But beauty was my first curse. It exposed me to the world and left me vulnerable to its consequences, forcing me into the restraints of a dangerous stereotype. *You cannot look like that and not expect attention. She is asking for it, surely? She must secretly want it, mustn't she? Because all women do, right?*

To put it plainly, my beauty was the catalyst for my downfall.

I discovered I was beautiful a little later than one normally would, because my isolated lifestyle had kept me wonderfully oblivious to it all. It makes me sad now, to think I will never have that youthful innocence again.

I remember the exact day it all began to change. I was seventeen summers old.

Theia had been out gathering food, whilst I busied myself with my usual duties, nattering away to Athena as I always did whilst alone. Suddenly, I had heard footsteps approaching behind me.

"Goddess," the stranger whispered. I can still picture him so clearly, his head was shaved, his mouth hidden by a thick knotted beard. His skin was bronzed and flecked with little white scars, each one hinting at a story waiting to be shared.

"Excuse me?" I stammered. I was not sure what to do, Theia usually dealt with visitors, so I was painfully inexperienced with the customs of *Xenia*, the ancient laws of hospitality which bound all beings together. It is one of the pleasanter rules of the Ancient World, yet one that seems to have been sadly forgotten these days.

"I am sorry," he laughed, running a hand over his bald head, "I thought you might have been Athena herself… Just, I have never seen such incredible beauty before." As his eyes locked onto mine I felt something loosen inside me. A warmth bloomed in my chest, spreading up to my cheeks. I did not realise it then, but it was the feeling of my innocence beginning to unravel. "I had heard rumour this land was cursed…but surely it cannot be cursed when a beauty such as yours walks upon it… May I ask your name?"

"Um…it is Medusa." I squirmed awkwardly. I could feel the weight of his gaze against my skin. Penetrating.

"Medusa," he repeated. I had never heard my name said like that before, charged by an unfamiliar intensity. It was as if this man had given my name a whole other meaning. I suddenly felt uneasy, though I wasn't sure why. All the man had done was call me beautiful, yet I could not deny my discomfort, it was right there, squirming in the pit of my stomach. I remained silent, not knowing how to ease this strange tension building between us. "Are you here all alone?" The look in the man's eyes shifted from admiration to something deeper, a look of hunger I had never seen before. I wish I could never see it again.

"Yes."

"Would you like me to keep you company?"

And suddenly, all at once, the pieces slotted into place and I understood. He *wanted* me. The realisation tightened in my chest, causing my cheeks to flush deeper. His desire suddenly felt like a tangible heat between us, burning my skin. He moved to take a step closer as a gasp caught in my lungs.

"Excuse me." I felt relief flood through me as Theia entered the temple, her walking stick clacking authoritatively against the ground. The man jumped, recoiling backwards as if he had been physically stung, the longing in his eyes quickly masked by a look of greasy innocence.

"Oh, hello, priestess." He cracked an amicable smile. Theia's eyes shifted to mine and an unspoken understanding passed between us.

"What do you want?" Theia snapped at him, seeing right through the man.

"Priestess, I have been travelling a long while...and I wanted a place to stay..."

"I can offer you food and shelter, but you are to leave the priestess alone, do you hear me?"

"What?"

"I know your type, boy. You reek of lust." I felt a swell of pride as tiny, frail Theia stepped up to the man, jabbing her walking stick into his chest. He looked stunned, as if he had never been told "no" in his life. Or perhaps he had, but had never really listened before. "Do you hear me?"

"I did not come here to be accused," he said, puffing out his chest.

"Let us leave the judgement to Athena, then. Though I doubt she'll take kindly to someone intent on desecrating her sacred space." Theia's voice hardened, her narrowed gaze unwavering.

"I have done nothing wrong," he replied defensively, a sudden tension in his jaw at the mention of the Goddess.

"Is that so?" Theia raised an eyebrow challengingly. An irritated noise escaped from the back of the man's throat, which he quickly tried to disguise with a tight, empty laugh.

"I meant no offence," he told Theia with thinly veiled contempt. "But I shall respect your wishes, priestess." His eyes then slithered across my body, lingering uncomfortably, before he finally relented and turned to leave.

Theia sighed as she watched him go, shaking her head slowly. When she finally turned to look at me, there was something in her eyes that unsettled me. She looked apologetic, mournful even. And that look confirmed what I had been fearing – this was only the beginning.

Everything changed once my innocence had been stripped from me, leaving my body bare for men to shamelessly ogle. Where I had once been excited by the rare company of others, now I was afraid of it. I dreaded our trips into town, as I knew I would be met with longing looks and hungry eyes, the kind that stained my skin, making my body no longer feel safe, no longer feel like my own. When you are beautiful everyone thinks you owe them something and that they have the right to simply reach out and take it – to stare, to touch, to claim. The world around me became ugly and frightening, as if a candle had been struck, illuminating the dangers I had been so blind to before.

43

I hated all of it and wanted nothing more than to hide away inside the temple, under Athena's protective gaze.

When I confided in my sisters about this, they had simply laughed.

"Well, Medusa has finally discovered she is beautiful." Euryale gave a dramatic sigh.

"I was hoping we could keep it from her for a little while longer." Stheno shook her head, but she was grinning despite herself.

"So was he cute? The guy at the temple?" Euryale leant forward eagerly, her eyes wide.

"No," I answered tersely, the memory prickling uneasily over my skin, "he just made me feel...uncomfortable."

"Oh, you just have to get over that part and then it's good!" she giggled.

"Why do you look so frightened, Medusa?" Stheno threw an arm round me and squeezed my shoulders. "You should be *enjoying* this, having men drooling at your feet."

"I preferred it when they ignored me," I muttered.

"You are beautiful Medusa, but you are still *so dull*," Stheno teased, giving me another squeeze. I could feel her feathers tickling against my skin.

"You'll learn to enjoy it one day, trust me." Euryale nodded reassuringly. I managed to return her smile, yet I could feel a familiar uneasiness churning away inside me.

Somehow, I knew this could only end badly.

Goodbyes.

Theia died the following year.

Her thread of life was cut, her fate sealed.

It was not a surprise to me; she had been deteriorating for a while. Chronos had finally caught up with her, as he always does. But even when you are expecting it, you cannot really ever prepare for something like that, can you?

I had never experienced death before that day and I had never known pain like it. I was so full of emotion, my entire body ached with it and yet I somehow felt completely empty, like a vast bottomless pit had opened up inside me.

My sisters found me at the foot of Athena's statue, sobbing. For the first time, they had no smirks or snarky remarks. Instead, they embraced me, their wings cocooning my shivering body, their feathers tickling against my tears. I had never been so grateful to have family, however small and dysfunctional.

Euryale and Stheno were as unfamiliar with death as I was; being immortal it was not in their sphere of reference. But they did their best to help me with the funeral arrangements. Theia had given me detailed instructions towards the end, so I knew exactly what needed to be done. We worked methodically to clean and anoint her body, whilst I tried to detach the woman I had known and loved from the cold, lifeless flesh beneath my hands. As I placed the customary coin inside Theia's slack mouth, I remember how it had seemed to eerily wink at me in the candlelight, causing a shiver to ripple over my skin. This coin was a vital part of the burial process, as it would serve as payment, allowing Theia's soul passage across the river Styx and into the world beyond.

Once Theia's body was prepared, my sisters left me alone to say my personal goodbyes. I know it was customary, back then, for women to sing and howl, to rip at their hair and beat their chests, to allow their misery to break free in a moment of raw and animalistic release. But, the truth is, I just couldn't. I couldn't utter a word, not even a 'thank you' or a 'goodbye'. I just stared numbly down at the collection of flesh and bones laid out before me. Because that's all bodies really are, once the soul has left, aren't they? Just flesh and bones.

Theia had asked to be cremated. My sisters built the funeral pyre and they held my hands as we watched the flames swallow up her small body. I could not watch for long. Instead, I chose to focus my gaze on the thick folds of smoke choking the evening sky, turning the blush of pink to a sinister grey.

I prayed to Athena as we watched Theia burn. I begged her to protect Theia, to guide her to the Underworld safely and please Gods let her rest peacefully. *Please be good to her, as she was to you.*

I have spotted Theia a few times down here in the beyond, though of course she does not recognise me anymore and I would prefer to keep things that way. I want her to remember me for how I was, in that brief pocket of time when I was young and carefree. I do not want her to see what I have become, or know what I did.

As dawn stretched her rosy fingers across the sky, I remember a resolution hardening inside me. The temple was my sole duty now and I had promised Theia I would live up to my name. *Protector.*

Needless to say, I was not able to keep that promise.

Visitor.

After Theia's death, I took my priestess duties even more seriously. I worked tirelessly day and night, not even taking time to see my sisters.

"Come on, Medusa, come hang out with us!" they implored, but I would only shake my head, without looking up from whatever task they had interrupted.

"Sorry, still work to be done."

"That's what you always say!"

In hindsight, I think I was throwing myself into work as a way to channel my grief. I cannot remember much from those days, time slipped past in a gloomy haze. My sisters grew bored and visited less. I suppose it was inevitable – immortals have a surprisingly short attention span, considering they have so much time to fill.

For a long while I had no visitors at all. I punctuated the endless silence by talking to Athena, as I had always done. But the one-sided conversations slowly descended into desperate pleas – *Please talk to me, please guide me, I need you.*

Of course, as always, Athena never replied.

I will admit, once or twice I considered packing up and leaving this life behind me. I imagined heading off with my sisters and exploring the wide world I knew so little about. But, though I fantasised about what that life could look like, I knew it would never become a reality. I could not dare betray Athena like that and I had promised Theia on her deathbed that I would never abandon the temple. I would stand by it always, as she had. Besides, as time passed I became content with my quiet life and even found myself enjoying the solitude – it was a sort of comfort, to be wrapped up safely in my own privacy, away from the unwanted attention of men. I told myself this was the life the Fates had decided for me and I was okay with that.

And that is when everything began to go wrong.

It started with a visitor, the first since Theia's death.

"Medusa?"

I was sitting out enjoying the last rays of evening sun, when the voice made me jolt out of my skin. It had been so long since I had heard another person, I thought I might have truly gone mad. I looked up as a shadow loomed over me, the unfamiliar figure etched by the dying sunlight. I shielded my eyes, squinting to try and make out the stranger.

"Well, well, well," he chuckled, his voice was light and playful, "they didn't exaggerate your beauty, did they?"

I rose to my feet immediately, my body instinctively tensing up from his words. As I blinked against the dark blotches in my vision, I slowly registered the stranger before me. He was slender for a man and appeared short, however as I stood up I realised he was substantially taller than me. His hair was in perfect blonde ringlets, which fell across his sparkling eyes – they were an unearthly shade of icy blue. He was handsome, disconcertingly so. He exuded a mischievous energy, it practically glowed from his skin. Somehow, I just knew he was a God, I could feel it in the way the air crackled around him. My eyes slipped down to his winged sandals and my suspicions were confirmed.

Hermes. The Trickster God.

The realisation caused my whole body to hum with a chaotic mixture of fear and awe. A God. But not just any God, an *Olympian*, one of the twelve elite deities who governed our world. Here he was, standing right in front of me! I had always hoped it would be Athena who would visit my temple, but coming face-to-face with any Olympian felt like an incredible honour...and danger. Of course, I knew all the myths of mortals who got themselves entangled with Gods – it seemed the mortals rarely came off well from the encounters. The Olympians were as unpredictable as they were powerful, so I knew I had to tread very carefully.

I fell to my knees.

"Hermes," I said, my voice trembling, "it is an honour to have you as a visitor."

"Oh, none of that." He waved his hand dismissively. "I'm just here on a casual visit, you know. Nothing formal." I rose to my feet, watching nervously as a mischievous smile played at his lips. My eyes met his and I found it hard to hold his gaze, it was unlike any other I had encountered. I was relieved to see he did not have that unsettling desire in his eyes, as the other men had. No, Hermes' gaze was quizzical and searching, as if my life was written plainly across my skin and he was amusedly examining each word. I had never felt so exposed before.

"I'm sorry I am not very presentable right now." I motioned to my messy hair and stained clothes. "Can I offer you a drink? Some food?"

"Wine," he said with a grin, "would be good."

After I had stopped my hands from trembling, I managed to retrieve the best wine we had – it was reserved for special libations to Athena. As I scurried back out of the temple I glanced at her statue and whispered, "I hope you don't mind." Her marble eyes glared out, unseeing, unresponsive.

49

When I came outside Hermes was sitting cross legged on the grass, playing his famous lyre. I stopped in my tracks, entranced by the sweet music dancing on the breeze around us. The sound shifted something inside me and I felt tears spring to my eyes. It was beautiful.

Hermes looked up, finally registering my presence. "Medusa, come sit with me." I felt a slight chill at hearing an Olympian say my name, it was thrilling yet terrifying.

"That was lovely," I breathed, as I lowered myself beside him, handing over the wine. I hoped he didn't notice how much my hands were trembling.

"Not bad, eh?" His perpetual grin broadened. "Would you like a go?" He handed the lyre out to me, cocking an eyebrow.

"Oh no, no, I don't know how." I panicked. "I've never played an instrument in my life... I'd butcher it." Hermes let out a musical laugh that seemed to echo all around us, his perfect curls quivering with the sound.

"Medusa, surely a beauty such as yours could not harm anything." His eyes glowed mischievously, his smile darkening. I sensed something unspoken hanging behind his words, but I had no idea what he could have meant. Of course, *now* I know. Hermes knew my fate and was mocking me for it, finding amusement in my obliviousness. The little prick.

"Here." He thrust the lyre into my hands. The instrument was so beautiful, even just touching it felt dangerous. "If you play half as lovely as you look, I think you'll do okay." He winked and leant back, propping himself up on his elbows as he sipped his wine, eyes settling on me. I shifted nervously under his gaze, holding the instrument awkwardly in my hands.

I was in an impossible situation: either I offended him by refusing to play, or I offended him by playing his instrument awfully. What was the lesser crime here?

"No, not like that. Hold it a little more upright. There you go."
He smirked round another mouthful of wine. He was loving this.

I tried to steady myself, but the fear was buzzing beneath my
skin, causing my hands to shake. I took a moment to breathe,
glancing again to check if Hermes was going to stop me, but he
just nodded expectantly. I held my breath and began to tactlessly
strum.

At first it sounded as awful as I had feared. It was as if
I was hurting the instrument, its strangled cries piercing the air.
I thought I should stop, but I was too afraid to do so without
Hermes' bidding. I glanced nervously at him, but he was just
looking off into the distance, that knowing smile still hovering
at his lips. Then, something remarkable happened. The dreadful
sound slipped effortlessly into a beautiful melody, much like the
one Hermes was playing before. I stared down incredulously as
my fingers deftly plucked the unfamiliar instrument. My hands
no longer felt like my own, but rather as if someone else was
commanding them. It was the strangest sensation I had ever felt;
mesmerising yet disturbing. Finally, the song came to a gentle
end, the last note hanging poignantly between us.

"See, you were pretty good," Hermes chuckled, taking the
lyre from me. I stared at my tingling hands, slowly wiggling
each finger to check they still worked. I knew I must have been
under some kind of spell and it made me uneasy to realise how
effortlessly Hermes could puppeteer me, like some toy. "You
should be more confident, Medusa. Perhaps then you will find
other hidden talents."

Hermes began to strum absentmindedly, humming an
unfamiliar melody under his breath. I watched and waited
patiently, I wasn't sure what for. He must have known I was

waiting for him to say or do something, but he just continued to idly play his lyre as if I were not there at all.

"You know they say this land is cursed," he finally said. His humming continued, but it was now disjointed from his body, coming alive in the playful breeze.

"Yes, I have heard it said," I replied carefully, not wanting to say the wrong thing.

"The rumours don't frighten you?" He cocked a playful eyebrow.

"Well, someone has to protect Athena's temple." I intertwined my fingers nervously in my lap.

"But you know what happened, don't you?"

"I've heard...stories." My mind flickered back to my sisters' dramatic retellings of the bloody destruction of the city.

"So you know it was destroyed by my dear uncle, Poseidon? One of his little tantrums." He gave a little chuckle. "He can be so *dramatic...* Mm, this is good wine!"

"You're welcome," I replied weakly.

"Tell me, have you heard of the Minotaur?" he suddenly asked. He regarded my blank expression slowly, then smacked his forehead. "Of course not! Silly me, he hasn't even been born yet, has he? I sometimes get my pasts, presents and futures mixed up. Don't you hate it when that happens?"

"You can see the future?"

"A little...though that's more Apollo's party trick." His eyes flickered to mine and I noticed something shift within them as he continued to speak. "Anyway, as I was saying, in years to come a creature will be born. A hideous thing, terribly ugly."

"The...Minotaur?"

"Exactly." Hermes' words caught alight as he spoke, sparked by some kind of excitable energy. "But you see, this Minotaur never did anything wrong. He was just the collateral damage, punishment for the actions of a greedy king. And yet, despite this, the creature will be treated as a monster its entire life, hated and condemned, forced into violence and ultimately...killed." He paused, his eyes studying mine, waiting for some kind of reaction.

"Why are you telling me this?" was all I could think to ask. Obviously now it all seems so infuriatingly clear, but I had been oblivious back then. How could I have known this myth would darkly parallel my own future?

"I just wondered what you thought of the story? An innocent creature forced to become a monster because of the actions of another..."

"Well..." I hesitated, suddenly concerned that this was perhaps some kind of divine test. After all, I knew it was not uncommon for the Gods to challenge mortals to test their piety. "If the punishment was the will of the Gods, then I believe it was the right decision."

"Even though the creature did not deserve it?"

"I trust the judgement of the Gods." I fought to hold his gaze, forcing myself not to look away.

"Hmm, quite." Something caught in Hermes' eyes, perhaps amusement? I could not be sure. "Remind me to ask you that again in a few months."

I let his foreboding words settle uneasily between us, uncertain how to adequately respond. Was he doubting my faith? I wanted to challenge him on this, but knew it would most likely be an unwise decision.

"Won't you drink with me?" he asked, his smile twitching. At my slight hesitation he added playfully, "You wouldn't refuse a God, would you?"

"No. Of course not…" I took the cup from him, flinching as my fingers sparked against his touch. I tried to ignore the intensity of his stare as I took a delicate sip.

"Not a fan?" Hermes chuckled at my grimace, as the acidic liquid burnt inside my throat.

"I've…never…drunk wine before," I spluttered, my cheeks burning hot with embarrassment.

"Oh really? You hide it so well…" Hermes teased. He then reached out and tipped the cup back up to my lips, his eyes narrowing. "The first sip is always the worst. Why not have another go?"

Reluctantly, I obliged. The wine's fiery sharpness soured against my tongue, though admittedly the taste was not as unbearable as the first time. An unfamiliar warmth began to glow inside my chest as I took another gulp, it felt strangely comforting.

"See? Not so bad is it?" Hermes grinned.

"Can I ask you something?" I said, surprising myself with my directness. Perhaps the wine had instilled a sudden confidence inside me, sedating my previous fears.

"Of course." Hermes sat up, crossing his legs and placing a palm on each knee.

"Why are you here?"

"I wanted to meet the famous Medusa, of course." His blue eyes shone, as if he had captured the last rays of sunlight inside them. "I am a big fan of your work…or else, I will be a big fan. One day."

"Famous?" I frowned, cradling the cup in my hands. "I am sorry but, I think you are mistaken, I am not famous…"

"Not yet, no. But soon." Hermes' teasing expression hardened into something more calculating. His eyes bore deep into mine, as if he were searching for something, I just didn't know what. I had to look away.

"What do you mean?" I breathed, feeling my chest tighten.

"I have probably said too much." Hermes gave an exaggerated gasp, his expression easing back to light playfulness. "Naughty me."

"But...I..."

"Anyway, I must go now," he said, rising abruptly, "you know how it is... So many lives to meddle with, so little time."

"But...but what about my future?" I stammered helplessly, scrambling to my feet.

"I wouldn't want to ruin the surprise now, would I?" Hermes snickered and bowed flamboyantly. "Well, Medusa, it has been my pleasure to meet you. I do look forward to watching your fate play out, it will be most...*interesting*." I stared at him numbly as he turned to leave, the wings at his ankles spluttering to life. He then added over his shoulder, "Oh and by the way, Poseidon wanted me to tell you he's got his eye on you!"

With that he flew off and I continued to watch until he became just a small smudge in the distance, disappearing from my life as quickly as he had crashed into it. I stayed like that for a while, as the sunset bled out across the horizon, draining all warmth from the evening air.

Trickster, indeed.

Hermes may seem harmless to you, but he is the sort of God who would hand you a candle in the darkness, whilst simultaneously tripping you over and then would stand back and laugh as the world burnt around him.

Hermes has also been known as the Messenger of the Gods, though believe me he is not the sort of person you would ever want to receive news from. You see, Hermes only shared the information he wanted to. He was continually stirring his giant bubbling pot of gossip – a little pinch of jealousy here, a sprinkle of hate there and don't forget a good dollop of paranoia. He loved nothing more than cooking up dramas and watching them unfold, with his feet kicked up and hands resting cockily behind his head. I can just imagine him sitting up on Mount Olympus and patting himself on the back after another good day of stirring up havoc.

But, despite all this, Hermes was by no means the worst of the Olympians. That I would soon discover.

In the wake of Hermes' visit I felt at a loss. The life I thought I knew had been unhinged, tilting precariously all around me. Countless questions mounted up, suffocating me. How would someone like me become famous? Was something bad going to happen to me? Why had he mentioned this Minotaur? And what did he mean by Poseidon having 'his eye' on me?

The questions clogged my mind, making it impossible to focus on anything else. I looked to Athena for help, as I always did. I knelt before her statue and pleaded for guidance. But, as usual, I was just met with that same cold, lifeless face.

Time passed but nothing happened. I felt constantly on edge, expecting at any moment for my life to be blown wildly off course. Or perhaps for Hermes to visit again and stir up further havoc inside my mind. But to my surprise, nothing changed. Life simply continued on as normal.

"Oh, Hermes is just a meddling little imp," Stheno said, when I told my sisters about my encounter with the God. It was the first time they had visited in weeks and I was relieved to have somebody to unload my anxieties on to. "Don't listen to a word he says."

"But he is a God, an Olympian."

"Yes, he's the *Trickster* God. He's famous for it," Euryale pointed out, as she absentmindedly plaited my hair. "Besides, being a God doesn't exempt them from lying. Gods lie all the time to get what they want."

"But why would he lie about this?"

"Because he knew you'd freak out, exactly like you're doing right now!" Stheno rolled her eyes. I'll admit, it was a relief to see how unfazed they were by it all.

"But why bother to visit me at all, then?"

"Perhaps he was bored." Euryale shrugged as her fingers worked methodically through my hair. It felt nice, to have actual physical contact again, it made me realise just how alone I had been before.

"He said something else as well." I flicked my gaze to each of them nervously. "He said Poseidon had 'his eye' on me..." Euryale and Stheno shared a look and then burst out laughing.

"Medusa," Stheno snorted, "Poseidon has his eye on anything with a pulse."

"She's right about that," Euryale giggled.

"So you really think I have nothing to worry about?" For the first time since Hermes' visit, I felt the sickening weight in my chest begin to lighten.

"Not at all," they said in unison.

And I believed them, because they were older and wiser than me, because I wanted so badly to and because I couldn't bear to think of the alternative.

Poseidon.

I come now to the darker chapter of my life.

There was a time when I could not bring myself to speak of my past, could not even think about it. But these days I am tired of running from the pieces of myself I cannot escape. Like broken shards I have tried to brush under the rug, I always know they are still there and that ultimately I will never be fully complete without them. I cannot escape my past because it is a part of who I am today. That is something that has taken me a long time to accept.

Perhaps in retelling the events, I will eventually find some kind of closure. Or perhaps I will not. Either way, I want the world to know what they did to me.

He came in the early morning.

I was on my usual morning walk along the seafront, enjoying the gentle sighing of the waves, as the world began to slowly wake up around me. It had been my favourite time of day, back then.

The sea was calm that day. I was skipping stones absent-mindedly, taking pleasure as they lightly kissed the water – one, two, three times. The world felt still and peaceful. It only took a moment for everything to change. The water started trembling, as if there were some kind of disturbance beneath the surface. Suddenly, the waves began to surge and swell restlessly, as a furious foamy bubbling began exactly where my last pebble had sunk. I watched, transfixed, as the water gurgled and gulped upwards, like a white frothing volcano. I had never seen anything like it. Then, all of a sudden, a mighty figure rose from the depths. I felt my heart nervously stutter as he began to walk forward, the waves crashing around him, like a herd of white horses cantering to shore. The figure gave an amicable wave with one hand and in the other he held a magnificent golden trident.

Poseidon. God of the Sea.

He reached land in no time at all, his great frame looming before me. He was huge. Broad and muscular, Poseidon was an entirely different build to the slight Hermes. His hair and beard were a mass of wild curls, flowing around him like the waves he commanded. He looked much older than Hermes; his features were somewhat weathered, yet he was still handsome, fiercely so. It was unsettling to see such unearthly beauty.

"Medusa, isn't it?" His voice was deep and rumbling. He let go of his trident and it was immediately swallowed up by the waves, vanishing instantly beneath the bubbling froth. I inhaled slowly and could taste the salt in the air around us.

"Poseidon…" I went to kneel before him, my whole body trembling as images of the devastated city swarmed my mind. Could it really have been his doing?

"None of that child." He cupped my chin, tilting my head up towards his. A smile hinted beneath his flowing beard. "You dropped this, by the way." He handed me the pebble I had thrown into the ocean and I felt my skin buzz from his touch. "Shall we walk?" I could do nothing but nod numbly, as I tucked the pebble away and followed after him along the shore.

His strides were heavy yet somehow graceful, as if he were not touching the ground at all. With each step the waves rushed to meet him, obediently bubbling up at his feet. I walked quietly beside him, terrified of the power that radiated from him. The air felt charged around us, fizzing with his godly energy. I had been amazed by Hermes' company, but Poseidon felt like an entirely different breed of God.

"I am a fan of your mother, you know," he said, after a while of walking in silence. I stole a look at him, but he was gazing out across the ocean.

"I am afraid I have never met my mother." I bit my lip nervously, afraid of saying anything that would risk upsetting him. I knew one wrong step could be fatal. How many had lost their lives to this God's short temper? My mind flickered back again to the ruined city.

"Really? Well, I am sorry about that." He sounded genuine. "She is a fearsome Goddess, your mother, she helps keep my seas dangerous…and I like that." He gave me a wink and despite myself I couldn't help but smile, feeling a small swell of pride in my chest. "She has lots of formidable children, creatures that mortals pray they shall never meet." A chuckle rumbled from deep in his chest, it sounded like thunder. "And then there is you." He stopped walking and turned to look directly at me.

"I am a disappointment to her," I murmured, my eyes flickering to his and away again. I found it hard to hold his powerful gaze.

Another boom of laughter from the God, as we carried on walking. "Well, she is a fool if she is disappointed in you," he said and I felt a small smile tug at the corner of my lips.

I'll admit it felt nice, to be admired by an Olympian. I had spent so much of my life feeling inadequate. I suppose I was also dazzled by his overwhelming presence, allowing his charm to cloud my better judgement, making me feel almost giddy. I remember thinking: could the rumours have been false all along? A foolish thought. But, having dedicated my entire life to the

Gods, I was desperate to see them in the best possible light, even if that meant blinding myself to reason.

"You are too kind." I blushed, glancing away.

"Do not be shy, child." He tilted his head towards me, forcing me to meet his gaze.

"I'm sorry," I murmured, feeling the heat lingering in my cheeks. "I have been alone for so long... I am not used to compliments."

"Well it is the truth... How could someone as lovely as you be a disappointment to anyone?" As he spoke, I felt something shift in the air around us. I tried desperately to ignore it, focusing on the ground before me, concentrating on each careful step. "Admittedly, I did not think it possible, for a Goddess such as your mother to create something so...exquisite." He reached out without warning and stroked my hair. His touch was surprisingly gentle, sending shivers across my skin. I caught his gaze and saw the ugly, unapologetic hunger that burned there. I can still see that look in his eyes, even now. I felt my previous giddiness instantly shrivel up inside me, replaced by a heavy realisation.

Not this. Please not this.

"Thank you," I whispered, looking away.

"I told you there is no need to be shy." His voice was a sickening mixture of amusement and condescension. "Although, you're even sweeter when you're shy." His words fell like cold stones in the pit of my stomach. He leant forward, so close the curls of his beard scratched my skin. My whole body stiffened. "Yes, very sweet," he murmured, mostly to himself. Then he let out another rumbling laugh and the waves crashed in chorus. "Well... Are you not going to compliment me? It is only polite to return a compliment, is it not?"

Panic caused my mind to go blank. What should I have said? If I were too complimentary he could perceive it as flirting. But if I was not complimentary enough I could risk angering him...

I tried to swallow, but my throat was too dry. "You are very... impressive," I managed, offering him a hesitant smile without meeting his gaze.

"Impressive, eh?" Poseidon mulled over the word, seemingly pleased. "And what is impressive about me?" He leaned in closer, grinning as he felt my body stiffen.

"I have...heard many stories of your impressiveness." I spoke softly in attempt to hide the trembling in my voice. "I was hoping you would tell me some yourself," I urged, desperate to stall the situation as much as possible. Poseidon's eyes shone at the prospect and before I could say another word, he had launched into one of his many famed myths.

"Well, you must have heard about the time I slayed my father to save all my siblings?" He gave a nonchalant shrug, but I could hear the eagerness lurking behind his words.

"I would love to hear it again. It would be an honour to hear it from you."

"Well, firstly, let me tell you that Zeus tells the story completely wrong..."

I feigned engagement as he talked, nodding and smiling at the appropriate moments. But inside my mind was racing, clutching helplessly at impossible ideas, desperately trying to form some kind of plan. How could I escape? I knew of Poseidon's lust, which was said to be even greater than his temper. I would be a fool to think he had come for any other reason, especially after Hermes' words – had Hermes been warning me? Or simply toying? I suppose that did not matter anymore, did it?

But how could I refuse a God without offending them? Surely I would be punished for rejecting him. But would he not respect the fact I was a virginal priestess to Athena? I had dedicated my life to serving the Gods, would he not appreciate that? Suddenly, an idea sparked in my head. *The temple.* It was a sacred and holy space, surely Poseidon would not dare to offend Athena by desecrating it? Had he not left it unharmed all those years before?

Like I have said, I was incredibly naïve back then.

"Did you know I am a priestess?" I asked Poseidon, when he had finally finished his story.

"Are you now?" He sounded amused by this, like when a child tells you what they want to be when they grow up.

"Yes. At the temple over there. I would be honoured to show you."

"If it would please you."

I remember the relief swelling in my chest as we approached the temple. With each step we took I felt myself getting closer to safety; it took all my willpower not to break out into a run.

The ruined city loomed ominously ahead of us, its long shadows reaching towards the temple like desperate fingers clawing the ground. I glanced towards Poseidon to try to decipher his reaction to the city, but he seemed entirely uninterested in our surroundings. His eyes remained locked on me, watching my every movement with a sickening smile catching at the corner of his lips. I turned my attention back to the temple, focusing my mind on getting inside, into the safety of Athena's protective embrace.

"Here we are!" I exclaimed as I finally stepped into the temple, my voice ragged with breathless relief. It felt as if I had reached my lifeboat at last. I tried to gather myself together, repeating over and over: *I'm safe now. Athena will protect me.*

"I remember this place." Poseidon entered slowly, his Godly presence making the temple look small and shabby. "Dear Athena's temple."

"Yes. Virginal Athena." I shot him a look, but he was too busy eyeing the space around him to notice. He looked less than impressed.

"I never liked her," he murmured absently, as he approached her statue. "She thinks herself above the rest of us because she is Zeus' *favourite*. She's an entitled bitch." I let out an audible gasp at his words, quickly throwing my hand to my mouth to try and catch the sound. Poseidon's eyes slipped into mine, he seemed amused by my shock.

"I still cannot fathom why those foolish mortals turned their backs on *me* for *her*," Poseidon continued, his voice darkening. "I took so much pleasure destroying that pathetic little city."

"It's…true then." The words escaped me before I could stop them.

"Of course." A smirk coiled around his lips like a snake ready to strike. "I obliterated every inch of that wretched little city… except for this temple." His smile began to twitch, hinting at a grimace. "It's always bothered me you know, leaving this temple untouched…" I felt his unspoken intent constricting the space between us, causing my breath to catch in my throat.

Had this been his aim all along, to come here and finish what he had started? Had I played right into his destructive plan? I found myself flailing helplessly for words, all I could manage was, "Athena…"

"What's wrong? Am I frightening you?" A dangerous mixture of passion and power curdled in Poseidon's eyes. "You are so lovely when you're scared." He took slow, deliberate steps towards me. "But you do not need to be afraid of me, child. I am not going to hurt you." I backed away until I was pressed against the wall. I could feel the sweat prickling down my spine.

Athena will protect me.

"Have you ever made love, Medusa?" The question chilled my insides, causing a cold panic to build inside me. It was in that moment I realised Poseidon did not intend to simply destroy the temple...he wanted to defile it.

"I'm...I'm a priestess," I stammered. "It's not... I'm not supposed to."

"But do you *want* to?" He was so close now, the heat of his body burning against me. The look in his eyes, that unbearable look. "I can tell you want to," he whispered. "It's okay, I won't tell if you won't."

Athena will protect me.

"We are in Athena's sacred temple." I was trying to stay calm, composed. "You cannot disrespect Athena."

"Oh Medusa, Medusa," he tutted, tugging at one of my curls idly. "Do you really think I care?" He then stroked my cheek, his hand large and hot against my skin. I winced as he traced his fingers along my jawline, down my neck, across my collarbone and finally to my breast. I recoiled away immediately.

"NO!" I shouted, surprised by the ferocity in my voice. Fear quickly clouded my mind – would he kill me for refusing him?

"No?" Poseidon only smirked.

"I'm sorry, I..."

"It's okay, I like women with a bit of fight in them." A violent hunger glowed in his eyes.

"You cannot do this." I was crying now, hot tears streaming down my cheeks, mingling with snot and sweat. "Athena... Athena will be angry with you."

Poseidon laughed emptily, his large frame trembling with the sound. "Well, fortunately I am not the one who promised myself to her, am I?"

I continued to beg him, desperate pleas ripping from my chest as blind panic overwhelmed me. But Poseidon did not listen to me, of course he did not. The Gods never do. I should have learnt that lesson by now, but I began to scream for Athena – *please Athena, save me, please!*

She was my only chance, my only hope.

Athena never answered.

I wish I could say I do not recall what happened next, I wish I could tell you it was all just a blur. But I remember everything. Every tiny detail.

At first, I had fought against him. But I was a drowning woman desperately trying to fight against the ocean, kicking and screaming hopelessly against the forceful waves – helpless. Inevitably, my mortal body grew weak and useless, until I was forced to stop resisting altogether and allow the ocean to swallow me up, to invade inside. A limp corpse being beaten and battered by the raging storm – lifeless.

I still remember the smell of salt on his skin as he surged into me, like the waves crashing onto shore, again and again and again…weathering down the rocks until there is nothing left.

I wished I would die.

At times, it hurt so much I thought I might.

When it was over, he did not say much. Why would he? He had gotten what he wanted and now I was just another used toy, dull and uninteresting. He was probably already thinking about his next conquest.

"Send Athena my love," I remember him saying before leaving.

I never saw Poseidon again.

As I lay on that cold, hard floor, I remember one thought running through my head: *Athena*.

Athena.

I have heard accounts that claim Poseidon and I were in love, that we were star-crossed lovers who started a secret affair, behind Athena's back. I think that is the version people are more comfortable with telling; it is politer, more palatable. The kind of conversation you could have around a dinner table.

I have even heard versions that claim that *I* was the seducer, luring in the unsuspecting Poseidon with my devious female ways. The sad thing is I am not even surprised by these lies. I was not the first woman to be blamed for a man's flaws and I certainly will not be the last.

I believe people prefer to tell these versions because it frees them of any accountability. They can remain blind to the realities of the world and instead transfer their collective guilt onto me – *it was her own fault!* One day, you will come to realise that people will always try and wriggle out of the uncomfortable truths, choosing instead to cushion their fragile egos with the lies they want to hear. Well, now I realise, it is our job to make them listen.

My sisters found me later that day, collapsed on the temple floor, staring at the small pebble in my hand.

"Medusa – who did this to you?" Stheno fumed, as they hovered round my crumpled body. I could not speak; I could not even cry.

"Oh, Medusa." Euryale tried to embraced me, but I recoiled away instantly. I could still feel him on me, as if I had been branded by his touch. It made me want to rip out of my skin, to tear the remnants of him from my body.

"Who was it Medusa?" Stheno was crouching by me now, her voice intent.

"Leave her be," Euryale whispered.

"Poseidon." His name was just a breath on my bruised lips.

Suddenly, the atmosphere grew heavy and swollen, as if a mighty thunderstorm were about to break out. The whole temple began to hum with an unearthly energy, I could feel it prickling over my skin. It was a feeling I knew all too well...

"You have to go." I managed to find my voice, pushing against my sisters. "You have to go *now*."

"Why? What's happening?" Euryale glanced around us, she could sense the change too.

"We are not going anywhere." Stheno looked me dead in the eyes.

I cannot tell you how, but I just knew it was her. And I knew she was angry.

"Please, you have to." I felt the panic rising inside me, like a bird beating in my chest, trying frantically to escape.

"We're not leaving you! Medusa, we're not-"

"How dare you?" The words cut through us, cold and clear like glass. They belonged to a voice I had never heard before and yet somehow still recognised.

Athena. The Goddess of War.

She was magnificent, terrifyingly so. Her beauty was strikingly harsh; the kind you would fear rather than desire. She was dressed in her full battle gear, the plume of her glittering helmet brushing against the ceiling as she glided forward. In her right hand she held a long spear, its blade winking threateningly in the light. She looked as if she were heading to war, a war she would undoubtedly win.

"Move," she hissed at my sisters as they positioned themselves protectively in front of me.

"Please, it's not her fault-" Stheno tried, but Athena cut her off instantly.

"Do you dare defy me?" She did not raise her voice; she did not have to. Even when speaking quietly Athena made the walls tremble.

Stheno and Euryale threw me a tortured look, their eyes filled with unspoken apologies as they shrunk backwards. "It's okay," I murmured to them softly.

"Get up," Athena ordered and I obeyed, tentatively finding my feet. My body was still so fragile, it hurt just to move. "Don't." Athena snapped, when my sisters instinctively moved forwards to help me. Once I was standing, she barked out another order, "Look at me."

I felt my lips trembling as I bit back my tears. I could not bear Athena seeing me like this, ruined and defiled. A disgrace. Yet I knew I could not disobey her direct command. As I reluctantly looked upwards I prayed that the ground would fall away beneath me so I could disappear in the depths of the earth.

Athena's grey eyes glowed in the half-gloom of the temple, as if they emitted a light of their own. They looked so familiar to me, those eyes I had spent my entire life gazing up at. But for the first time ever, they were staring right back at me. I felt a sudden rush of emotion overwhelm me, threatening to spill over.

"Medusa, my priestess," she said and I remember feeling a fragile spark of hope strike somewhere inside me.

"Athena."

"Tell me something." She inclined her head slightly, her grey eyes burning brightly. "Did you take *pleasure* in defiling my temple?" Her question dripped with malice, extinguishing my hope immediately. "Did you *relish* disrespecting me?"

"Athena, it was not my fault, Poseidon…" I fought to keep my voice level. "He forced himself on me… I was powerless against him… I tried to stop him."

Athena made a disgusted noise at the back of her throat. "I am so tired of women not taking responsibility. Have some self-respect."

"I took him here because I thought I would be safe."

"So, you admit that you brought him here voluntarily?" Her voice had a dangerous edge to it. "You are a vile creature."

"No, it's not like that! Please, I had no choice, I thought I would be protected here… I called to you for help…"

"Are you trying to blame me now, you little whore?" Her fury radiated from her body, electrifying the air around us.

"No, no, I'm not at all." I felt the fear grip my insides. "I just… I did not mean to… I am sorry."

"You are sorry?" Athena gave an empty laugh. "Do you really think your pathetic apology is enough?"

I opened my mouth to try to reason with her again, but suddenly an overwhelming sense of defeat descended over me, draining the fight from my body. Just as I had with Poseidon, I felt myself giving in and letting go. I remember hearing Theia's words faintly echoing in my mind: *what will be will always be.* Suddenly, it all became clear to me, that to fight against this would only prolong the inevitable. The Fates had already decided, had they not? Besides, I thought, Athena's punishment could not be any worse than what I had already endured. Could it?

"No," I murmured, bowing my head. "I deserve to be punished."

"No, Medusa!" Stheno suddenly rushed forward, moving in between myself and Athena. "Can you not see the girl was *raped*, can you really be so blind?"

"It's not her fault, please don't hurt her." That was Euryale, appearing beside Stheno now.

"You should be punishing Poseidon, not Medusa." Stheno's voice was surprisingly strong in the face of an Olympian. "Medusa has never done a thing wrong in her life, all she has ever done is worship *you*!"

"She's a good person," Euryale enthused, looking a little more nervous under Athena's penetrating glare.

I remember feeling a muddle of fear and love battling inside me, as I watched my sisters risk everything to protect me. I realised in that moment that despite all their mocking and teasing and seeming indifference, they loved me... They really, truly loved me.

A slight pause followed, as Athena glanced between each of us. Was she reconsidering her verdict? That small gleam of hope had not entirely been lost inside me. "Fine," she said flatly, "I will punish all three of you."

"No!" The breathless word escaped me. "Please do not harm my sisters, they are just trying—"

"I have had enough of you all," Athena sighed irritably, bashing her spear on the ground to silence us. "Do you really think I have nothing better to do than argue with the likes of you?" She posed it like a question, but we knew better than to answer. As Athena spoke I felt Euryale and Stheno's hands slip into mine; they squeezed tightly, but I was so numbed by fear I could barely even feel it. "You deserve this, all three of you."

Athena then widened her arms and as she did so the shadows began to come alive around us, as an almighty storm started to rage outside, hammering relentlessly against the temple's walls. Athena's voice cut cleanly across the howling wind. "Medusa, you will become as repulsive as your actions. Never again will you use your temptress ways, for you will be so hideous that no man will ever be able to look at you again." The storm was getting louder now, making the ground beneath us tremble. "For trying to defy me, Euryale and Stheno, you will meet the same hideous fate as your sister. Maybe next time you will think twice before questioning the judgement of an Olympian."

She clapped her hands once and the sound reverberated outwards, cutting into my body like a blade. There was a moment of quiet, I remember looking down to see if I had actually been wounded, but there was nothing there, nothing at all. Then the blinding pain hit me, engulfing my entire body, ripping from the inside out. I could hear Euryale and Stheno screaming. I tried to reach out to them but the pain was too much. It felt as if my body were being broken apart; every muscle torn, every bone shattered, my skin was on fire. But, as I writhed in agony, the most disturbing thing I remember were those grey eyes smiling.

And then, the world went dark.

The Gods.

I want to just take a moment to tell you that Poseidon was never punished for his actions. I doubt Athena ever even mentioned it to him. Whilst my life was irrevocably ruined, Poseidon continued on as normal – taking whatever he wanted at whatever the cost and never being held accountable. I wish I could tell you I was his only victim, but there were so many others, I have lost count. And how I wish this vile behaviour had died out with our world, but I watch, outraged yet not entirely surprised, as the same tragedy echoes throughout generations, leaving an endless trail of broken victims and unscathed perpetrators.

At least one thing has changed, though. The Gods no longer roam the Earth. How I envy modernity for that. You might wonder, where are they now? I can assure you they still exist, of course they do, it is all part of the curse of immortality. But as mankind slowly found its independence and lost interest in the Gods, they lost their control and with it their power. Now they waste away on Mount Olympus, waiting endlessly for the day they might become relevant again. But the world does not want them anymore and why would they? They are nobodies now. They are nothing.

You hear that Athena? You are nothing.

I often wonder what would have happened if the life the Fates had drawn out for me had been woven differently. I frequently torture

myself with the endless possibilities of how things could have turned out. There is one scenario that sticks in my head, like a splinter
I just cannot get rid of – what if Athena had acted differently? What
if she had seen me as a victim, instead of the culprit? What if she
had entered the temple that day and embraced me, cried with me,
held me like my own mother never had? And what if she had faced
Poseidon, called him out on his vile actions and shamed him in
front of the other Olympians – would he have listened? Would he
have cared? Would other mortals have been spared from his violent
lust?

I am aware this alternate reality is just a naïve fantasy – Athena
is not capable of such compassion towards other women. In fact,
I have reason to believe Athena hated women altogether. Perhaps
because she never identified as one herself. Born from the head
of Zeus, in full battle gear, Athena never had the gentle touch of
a mother, or the softness of youth. She entered the world a cold
warrior and that is how she will forever be. However, I must add
that she was not entirely devoid of feeling. She did have a certain
fondness for heroes, I think because they were the only mortals she
felt an affinity with. Heroes were men chosen by the Fates to live
courageous and valiant lives, faced with epic adventures on their
quest for *kleos,* glory. Athena would all too readily save her beloved
heroes from the wrath of the other Olympians. But, of course, it
was *far* too much to expect her to save a pious, vulnerable, young
woman like me.

I also often wonder how different my life would have been if I
were born a man. Would Athena have protected me then? Would
Poseidon have respected me? I claimed earlier that beauty was my
first curse, but perhaps it was actually being born a woman.

One of the heroes that Athena admired and aided was the
man who would ultimately kill me. Perseus. Perhaps you have

heard of him? You might be thinking I am a man-hater (and could you really blame me?). But I must confess, I do not hate *all* men. I have some exceptions, albeit few. Perseus is one of those. This might come as a surprise to you, considering he cut off my head and all. But again, I am jumping ahead of myself.

We will get to Perseus a little later.

Monster.

I woke to the smell of smoke.

Great wafts of it seeped into my lungs, forcing me awake. When I opened my eyes the world around me was on fire. Giant flames danced before my eyes, their flickering fingers reaching out towards me.

"Medusa!" I heard Stheno and Euryale calling out. I opened my mouth to respond, but I could only retch helplessly. The heat blistered against my skin, but it was nothing compared to the smoke. I could feel it invading my entire body, clogging my insides, suffocating me. "Medusa!"

I tried to stand up, but my body grew sluggish, as if my limbs were weighed down by some invisible force. The world started to slip out of focus, shimmering around the edges and then blurring completely. I blinked to try to focus my vision, but I could already feel darkness slowly enfolding me in its cold embrace. I stopped fighting against it and I remember thinking how freeing it would feel to just let go…

Suddenly, there was a force around my arms, dragging me backwards. I could just make out my sisters' faces through the smoke; they were shouting something at me, but all I could hear was the blood rushing in my ears. I must have lost consciousness, because when I opened my eyes I could see the sky above me. I squinted up at the clouds. They looked so innocent and ordinary, as if nothing at all had happened, as if my world had not just been ripped apart. I blinked slowly, uncertain as to whether I was alive or dead. *Does it matter?* I remember thinking.

I realised I could still smell the smoke and hear the crackling of the flames. When I sat up, I finally registered what was happening. The temple was on fire. Every inch of it was engulfed in flames, burning with an unnatural ferocity. I knew it was Athena's doing, though she was nowhere to be seen now. Soon there would be nothing left, it would be reduced to dust just like the rest of the city. The temple that had withstood so much had finally fallen…because of me.

What did I feel as I watched the temple burn? I cannot really put it into words, if I am honest. It was my only home, my only purpose, the one thing I had promised Theia I would protect. And yet, it was also the place where Poseidon had defiled me, the place where I had wasted my whole life dedicating myself to a callous, uncaring Goddess.

Let it burn. I heard an unfamiliar voice whispering in my ear, soft and sinister. Something was tickling at my temples. *And let the old Medusa burn with it.*

"Medusa, are you okay?" I suddenly realised Euryale was crouching behind me, her voice trembling. I couldn't speak, I couldn't even look at her. The depth of my guilt was unbearable.

Guilt is for the weak. That voice again, hissing gently. *We are above that. We are better than that. We are powerful now.*

"Medusa, look what Athena has done to us!" Euryale sounded as if she were close to tears; I had never seen her cry before. In the distance, I could hear Stheno howling with anger; she sounded inhuman.

Go on, the voice urged, *look.*

Reluctantly, I turned to face my sister.

I have seen many different depictions of my sisters and me. Some are admittedly fairly accurate, whilst others are so far off the mark it is almost comical. The ones that make me laugh the most are where we are depicted as beautiful women, with snakes wrapped seductively around us. Honestly, people will try to sexualise anything, won't they? Well, I can assure you – we were not beautiful.

We were hideous.

I stared silently at Euryale and then looked down at myself. Her body, like my own, was the texture of snake skin, scaled and glistening. Euryale's face was fearsome, made up of sharp edges and severe details. Her eyes were inky dark pools, her black gums filled with rows of sharp, tiny teeth. Her hair was thin and lank on her head, as if it had been burnt in the flames. The only thing left unchanged were her wings, still darkly magnificent.

Have you seen your own? The voice tickled in my ear and suddenly I felt it, that new, unfamiliar weight quivering on my back. Could it be? *Yes.* The voice replied. *Why not try them out?*

"I do not deserve them," I muttered to myself, "I do not deserve anything."

Self-pitying is beneath us, the voice replied, suddenly hot with anger.

"I am hideous." Euryale was weeping now and I felt the guilt burning deep inside me. It was my fault. All of it. I was like a poison, infecting everything I touched. I had ruined everything I ever cared about.

"Euryale…" I began, but found no words. What could I say? How could I ever apologise for this? Words would never be enough.

"Medusa, wait!" Euryale called after me, but I had already broken into a run. I do not know what possessed me, but I knew

I just had to get away, away from my sisters, away from the temple, from this cursed patch of land. I did not stop running, hurtling straight towards the cliff edge and then, without hesitation, I threw myself off.

The wind whistled past me as I plunged towards the ocean. It faintly reminded me of the first time I had met my sisters. A dark part of me wondered if I should just let myself continue falling, was that all I deserved?

Fly! The voice ordered in my ear and suddenly I felt my wings unfurl, beating against the wind until I was soaring upwards. It felt incredible, but the feeling was quickly soured by the overwhelming guilt – I did not deserve to feel incredible, I did not deserve to feel anything.

I glided over the ocean, watching the restless waves churn beneath me. The sight of them made me nauseous, bringing back all too recent memories. But I did not turn back, I could not. I did not know where I was heading, I just knew I had to get away from it all.

I flew through the night and all the next day. I flew until my lungs burned and my wings began to seize up, though this pain was a welcome distraction from my inner torment. I remember the voice in my ear telling me to stop, but I could not. I had to keep going. That was all I could focus my mind on.

Eventually, my wings gave out in exhaustion and I crashed down onto an unfamiliar island, though I barely felt the impact. I lay still for a few moments, my whole body burning as I gasped for air. Beneath me, the dirt felt powdery and warm, the cracks in the dry earth twisting outwards like exposed veins.

"Are you alright…?" A voice sounded from a little way off. My body immediately went rigid, fear draining my mind of all reason. "Do you need help?"

I looked up to see a worn-looking shepherd standing further up the island; I had to squint to make him out against the dusty landscape. A young boy was scrambling aimlessly on the rocks beside him, seemingly unaware of me. As soon as the shepherd registered my appearance his entire demeanour changed, hardening with a look of repulsed fear. He quickly moved to wrench his son behind him.

"What are you? What do you want?" The shepherd's voice was now sharp.

"I mean no harm," I whispered, lowering my eyes. I could not meet his gaze, I could not bear to see the disgust that burned there.

Look him in the eyes, Medusa.

Do it. Go on.

Look.

"No!" I silently told the voice.

The shepherd crouched down and murmured something to the young boy, before ushering him off up the hill. As the boy quickly scrambled off, the man turned to me and I spied a small dagger winking in his right hand.

"Please, I…"

"Get away!" He held the weapon out, swiping it madly like you might do to scare off a wild animal. "Get away, you beast!"

Look him in the eyes, Medusa!

Do it! Now!

I unfurled my wings and began to beat them against the ground, ignoring the voice and my screaming muscles as I surged upwards into the air. The shepherd shrank away beneath me, but continued to wave his dagger, shouting vile profanities. In the distance, I saw a pack of men led triumphantly by the small child – they were holding up sinister-looking weapons and jeering

81

excitedly. They were coming to hunt me, to slaughter me like some kind of animal...like a monster.

A powerful monster, Medusa.

Do not be afraid of who you are.

"Get out of my head!" I cried furiously, hot tears blurring my vision as I soared higher. I wanted to get as far away from the island as my wings could carry me, though no matter the distance between us, I could still hear the shepherd's fearful disgust ringing in my ears.

Do not listen to him, Medusa.

Listen to us.

Eventually, I caught sight of a cave tucked against a sheer cliff edge. No human could possibly live here, I assured myself as I drew closer, feeling the flecks of sea salt spray against my skin. The smell made my stomach knot. It made me think of *him*.

The cave's inky darkness was cool and inviting as I landed carefully inside. I took one step and my body immediately gave out, collapsing heavily into the reassuring shadows. I felt the impact of the cold floor against my face, but the pain felt oddly dull and distant. I did not try to get up. What would be the point? Why would I want to?

You are stronger than this Medusa, stop it.

Get up, Medusa.

Listen...

"Leave me alone!" I shouted at the voice and to my relief it finally went quiet.

I welcomed the silence that followed.

I was alone at last.

Mother.

Time passed, but I barely noticed it.

I was wallowing in my pain, bathing myself in it like a wounded animal. I tended to my misery like a little pet. It was the only companion I wanted. It is hard to explain, but I did not want to be happy, in all honesty I was afraid of it – with happiness came risk, risk of failing, risk of losing it all. Misery felt safer, it felt familiar. There are no expectations when you are sad.

I lay in that cave for a long while. I felt safe blanketed by the heavy shadows, wrapped up tightly in that cold gloominess. I remember wishing I could just lose myself within the darkness and disappear completely. Left alone forever. Though I gradually came to realise I was not alone, not exactly. You see, at times I could feel a strange stirring around my temples; it slithered and writhed, hissing softly. Something was alive in the shadows.

Medusa… Listen to us…

Take a look… Go on…

Medusa… Look at yourself…

I assumed I had gone mad and this was just a symptom of my insanity, so I tried to simply ignore it. Besides, why would I want to look at myself? I knew what I had become and to see my hideous self would be just another reminder of what I had done. Just as Athena had said: *you will be cursed to become as repulsive as your actions.*

The guilt overwhelmed me, I could feel it squirming in the pit of my stomach constantly. I felt guilty for everything – for destroying Theia's beloved temple, for ruining my sisters' lives, for disappointing the Goddess I had idolised since childhood. I hate to admit it now, but I even felt guilty for Poseidon's actions. My mind became my worst enemy, endlessly playing out our encounter, over and over and over, hunting for any scrap of detail I could use to feed that guilt, like picking at a wound you just cannot let heal. I *had* invited him to the temple, hadn't I? I had thought him handsome too and even called him 'impressive'. I had let him put his hands on me. I had been reluctant to say 'no'… Had I really been asking for it? Had I somehow encouraged Poseidon? I could hear Athena's voice, running circles in my mind: *tired of women not taking responsibility…you little whore… You took your lover to my temple to purposefully offend me…* Had she been right?

It pains me to think of the blame I blindly accepted. But when you are in that kind of broken state, it is impossible to not let the darkness seep in through the cracks. I wish I could reach across the folds of time and call out to that old Medusa. I wish I could scream at her: *YOU ARE NOT GUILTY.* I would hold her in my arms and tell her *YOU DO NOT DESERVE THIS, YOU NEVER DESERVED ANY OF THIS.* Do you know, nobody has ever said those words to me? It was just something I had to figure out for myself, eventually. But let me tell you, the most powerful revelations are the ones we discover for ourselves.

I am not sure how much time passed. I did not eat; I did not drink. I am surprised I did not die, if I am honest. Each day the voice inside my head persisted and each day I ignored it.

Medusa. Go and look. Go.

"Go away!" I would cry.

Medusa, listen...

"LEAVE ME BE!"

But eventually, I succumbed. I do not know why, perhaps there was a small part of me that actually wanted to live. Or perhaps the voice had finally just got to me, infecting my mind and forcing my hand. Either way, I eventually dragged myself from the cave and out into the frightening world.

The moon Goddess, Selene, was high in the sky, her chariot spilling its silvery glow across the dark ocean. The glimmering waves looked beautiful, but the sound of them only made me shudder, bringing back memories of his touch. I felt sick.

I carefully clambered my way down to the water's edge, urged on by the bodiless voice. *Over there,* it hissed and I turned to see a small rock pool, illuminated in the moonlight. I staggered over and collapsed beside it, like a dying animal coming for its final drink.

Look, Medusa. Look.

I gingerly hoisted myself up and gazed into the clear, still water. An unfamiliar face stared back. It was the face of a monster, the face of a Gorgon. What did I think, when I finally saw myself that very first time? Honestly, I think my first thought was that at least my sisters and I would look related now. Though their eyes had been dark, whereas mine were entirely white, clouded and eerie. But what had caught my attention the most was my hair... It was *alive*, writhing and wriggling around my head.

I will admit, the snakes were an interesting touch. I have never really known why Athena incorporated them into my monstrous look, though I have my theories about her dark intentions. Perhaps it was simply because the Gods cannot help but add a touch of the dramatic to whatever they do.

I stared, mesmerised at my reflection and the snakes stared back, their narrow little eyes glinting in the moonlight, sharp tongues flickering. They were hideous and wonderful.

See, Medusa. We are magnificent. Suddenly, I realised. That voice…it was *their* voice…it had been them all along. The snakes…my snakes.

"Who are you?" I asked them softly.

We are you. And you are us, the snakes whispered back as they gently stirred around me, dipping towards the water's surface.

"But why… How?"

Look, they interrupted in unison, *a visitor…*

A visitor? The word made me flinch and a familiar icy fear shot through me. I envisioned the shepherd flanked by his comrades, holding their weapons aloft as they charged at me. I did not want them to look at me, I did not want anyone to ever look at me again. I staggered to my feet, wondering how quickly I could scramble back to the safety of the cave. But that is when I saw her, standing in the ocean, the waves calmly lapping around her waist. She turned to look at me, just as the snakes' whisper flickered in my ear: *Mother.*

As she waded her way to the shore I felt myself being inexplicably drawn towards her, despite my better judgement.

"Hello, child," she said when we reached one another. Her face was turned upwards, the delicate moonlight etched against her harsh features.

"Mother?" I breathed. I could hardly dare believe it.

"It has been a while." Her eyes found mine and they reminded me of my sisters'. She did not smile, but there was something in her gaze that made a lump of emotion rise in my throat. *My mother.*

She was not beautiful, but she was striking. Being a Goddess, she had that same unnerving air of power about her, though hers was more of a subtle glow, compared with the overwhelming presence of the Olympians. Her skin was made up of iridescent fish scales, which glittered brilliantly in the moonlight. Crustaceans and algae clung to her skeletal body, as if to the underside of a weathered ship. Her dark hair was damp and glistening, entangled with seaweed and constantly flowing around her, giving the impression she was floating underwater even when on land. Her mouth was just a thin slash, permanently downturned.

"You look different." She regarded me, the ghost of a smile hovering at her lips. I felt my snakes begin to stir at my temples, hissing softly.

"A lot has happened," was all I could manage. That familiar shame began to burn inside me, forcing me to turn away from her. I had wanted my whole life to meet my mother and now I could not even look at her. "I didn't want you to see me like this…"

"Why, child?" Her voice was cold, yet not unkind.

"Because I am a disgrace…" I looked down at my body. "This is a punishment. This is a reminder of my guilt."

"I do not see a punishment."

"But look at me – I am hideous." I glanced upwards and her eyes locked onto mine, unwavering.

"You look powerful to me."

"Powerful?" The word surprised me. I had never been powerful in my entire life.

Powerful. The snakes chorused in my ear. *Yes, powerful Medusa.*

"Listen to me, Medusa." Her voice was firmer now, edged with severity. "You can choose to see this as a punishment and spend your days wallowing in self-pity, if that's what you want. Or, you can see this for what actually it is…an opportunity."

"An opportunity?"

"Yes." Her eyes glowed. "An opportunity to be powerful and feared. An opportunity to right the wrongs the world has forced on you." As she spoke, I felt her words igniting something in my veins – an unfamiliar sensation tingled through me.

Powerful.

Feared.

Revenge.

"You could do so much, Medusa." She reached out and placed a hand on my shoulder; the snakes' tongues flickered in greeting at her cold touch. The simple gesture felt overwhelming and I had to hold back my tears. *Was my mother finally accepting me? Even after everything I had done?*

"I… I'm not sure if I can…"

"The question is not whether you can or cannot, Medusa," she cut me off smoothly. "The question is: how do you want the world to remember you? As the pathetic victim of Poseidon and Athena? Or as a powerful woman who brought revenge to her enemies?"

"But…"

"Medusa!" Her voice had risen now, amplified by the sudden crashing of the waves around us. "Where is the fight in you, child? Are you not angry at what they did to you? Are you not furious?"

Listen to her, Medusa.

"Have you forgotten already what Poseidon took from you?"

Let it out.

"Or what Athena forced on you?"

Go on, Medusa.

"Or are you just a pathetic little victim after all?"

"NO!" The word ripped out like an animalistic scream, as I felt something cracking open inside me. Under all the suffocating misery and guilt, I finally felt the anger that had been bubbling quietly, hot and impatient. Now that rage was surging upwards, invading every inch of my body, overwhelming me, like a phoenix rising from the ashes.

"Good." An ominous smile curled at my mother's lips. She could see my potential coiled within my fury, an animal waiting to strike. "Now let us put that anger to use, shall we?" She cast her gaze towards the ocean and pointed at a small blot against the horizon. "You see that ship there? It is full of sailors returning from their travels. Mortal men who have indulged their ugly appetites with raping and pillaging, leaving nothing behind but a wake of destruction." She turned to me and her smile grew wider, revealing her sharp jagged teeth. "I think you ought to pay them a visit, don't you?"

"Yes, mother." I nodded, unfurling my wings and taking off into the dark sky without hesitation, my body fuelled by the anger that had consumed me.

I felt powerful.

I felt reborn.

Punisher.

I landed silently on the ship, obscured by the moon-cast shadows. It was quiet on deck, I assumed most of the crew must have been sleeping. The only sound I could hear was the gentle shushing of the waves and the creaking of oars, as the men below deck rowed tirelessly through the night.

A little way ahead, I made out a figure lolling against the mast. As I advanced he swung round clumsily, sloshing his wine across his shirt. Drunk and pathetic. If I am completely honest, I have no idea what my plan was as I approached that man. I was driven blindly by the anger humming inside me, could feel it singing through my veins. The snakes were also urging me on, their slithery voices overlapping and intertwining excitedly in my ear.

They deserve to die, Medusa.

They deserve to suffer.

Like you did.

Make them suffer.

Do it, Medusa.

Show them who you are.

"Who goes there?" The man's tongue stumbled over the syllables.

Tell him to look at you, Medusa.

Make him look at you.

"Why not take a look?" My voice sounded different – darker, stronger. I sounded powerful.

The man held out his torch and in the light of the dancing flames I could see he was young, younger than I had expected – he barely had any hair on his chin. I suddenly hesitated as my anger faltered, but the snakes rebelled against me.

No, Medusa! Think of what he will turn into.

Think of what he will become. Make your mother proud.

Take your revenge. Do it!

I was still hidden in the shadows as I deliberated over my next move. The man squinted and stepped closer and that is when I noticed the scratch marks around his neck. Somehow, I just knew they were the marks of someone who had been trying to escape, someone who had been trying to force him off them. The marks of a frightened woman. In that moment, I was immediately transported back to that cold temple floor, feeling the full force of Poseidon on top of me as I fought helplessly against him, crying out for Athena…

He deserves to die like the rest of them.

In hindsight, I suppose those marks could have been scratches from anyone or anything – but in that moment I was so sure, so certain. Nothing could have swayed my decision to end this man's life.

Punish him, Medusa! Do it!

Driven forward by the snakes' encouragement, I stepped into the delicate pool of light and raised my hands ready to strike. Looking back now, my reckless confidence seems almost laughable. I had never fought anyone in my life, I had never even raised a finger against someone. Yet there I was, weaponless and painfully inexperienced, preparing to fight my way through a ship of men who were most likely all armed. I suppose my hatred was blinding me from my better judgement, my confidence spurred on by the encouragement of the snakes. Besides, when you truly feel you have nothing left to lose it strips you of any fear.

Look at him, Medusa.
Stare into his eyes.
Look! Look!

The man immediately swung out his sword when he saw me, staggering slightly as he did so. I dodged, watching as he steadied himself and prepared for another blundering swing.

Look, Medusa. Look!

As he stepped forward to strike again, I locked my eyes on to his and felt the strangest sensation overcome me. A sharp coldness cut through my temples and my peripheral vision darkened, narrowing the world around me, as if I were suddenly staring through a tunnel – all I could see ahead were the man's eyes. I can still picture them, a mossy green colour, flecked with hazel. It is funny, those little details that stay with us, isn't it?

The man did not even have time to scream. As I gazed into his eyes, I saw his shock curdle with fear and then harden into something else entirely, turning dull and unresponsive, the life draining out until all I was staring at was cold stone. I blinked and felt the world readjust into sharp focus around me. When I looked back at the man he was entirely frozen, solid and motionless. His mouth was half open, forever held in a silent scream. Stunned, I stepped forward and touched his arm, it was cold and hard. He was completely stone.

He was my first victim.
Do you see, Medusa?
Do you see what you can do?
Do you see how powerful you are?

"What is going on? What is that *thing*?" a voice yelled, as I heard footsteps rushing towards me.

Show them, Medusa.

Show them what you can do.

I could sense the men surrounding me and heard the sinister, unfamiliar sound of unsheathing swords. But I did not acknowledge them, I was utterly engrossed by the stone figure before me. You could still see the terror etched into his stony features. I reached out to touch his face, realizing that he would be forever encapsulated in that moment of pure fear. I was transfixed, I had never seen a man so afraid before – lust, longing, hunger, power, those were what I associated with the male gaze. But never fear.

Beautiful is it not? the snakes sang in my ear. *Now show the rest of them.*

I realised the men around me were shouting now.

"What's she done to him?"

"The bitch turned him to stone!"

"She's some kind of monster, just look at her…"

"She's a creature from the Underworld…"

Tell them who you are.

"I am Medusa," I spoke calmly, continuing to stare into the lifeless eyes of my first ever victim.

"Medusa, what is a Medusa?"

"Her head will make us a pretty penny."

"Those wings too."

"Just kill the bitch!"

They advanced forwards, their circle tightening around me. There must have been over a dozen of them surrounding me and for the briefest moment I hesitated, feeling the ugly voice of self-doubt crawl into my ear. How had I managed to kill the man before? What if I could not do it again?

Just look at them, Medusa. Trust us.
Trust yourself.
Just look.

I turned to meet them, casting my deathly gaze across each man in turn. I felt the same coldness cutting through me as I looked into each pair of defiant eyes. The effect was almost instantaneous, it happened so quickly I doubt they even realised what was happening. The fools. Within seconds, I was surrounded by motionless statues, frozen mid-action, weapons held aloft to strike me down. They would never get the chance. They would forever be trapped in the moment of their final failure.

Do you see now, Medusa?
Do you see how powerful you are?

I walked up to one of my statues; his sword was held above his head, his face frozen in a look of pure animalistic blood-lust. I flicked his sword and watched a crack spark along the length of the weapon. I then did something I had not done in the longest time…

I laughed.

A loud, ominous laugh ripping from deep inside me, rising up into the dark sky above. It felt like pure release.

"Excellent work, Medusa." My mother appeared suddenly beside me, a pool of water gathering at her feet. She was inspecting the statues, a cold smile peeling back her thin lips. "I am impressed."

"There are others," I said breathlessly, feeling the power hum inside me, "other men below deck."

"Yes, you are right." My mother looked me right in the eyes.

"Let us kill them together, mother. You and I…"

"You have done enough for tonight, Medusa," Her voice sounded final, uncompromising. "You want this ship to reach the port. You want these men to be found."

"But why?"

"So that the tale of Medusa's wrath will spread and the world will learn to fear you."

Fear me... The idea was intoxicating. I could feel the snakes' agitated excitement, their cold, slithering bodies like a tangled crown atop my head.

Fear the powerful Medusa!

No longer Medusa the victim.

Never again, that Medusa is gone. Dead.

Long live powerful Medusa!

"You have done well, my child." My mother nodded slowly and I felt an unfamiliar thrill buzzing beneath my skin.

She was pleased with me, proud even. But of course she was. My mother had finally gotten rid of her ordinary mortal child. She finally had her monster.

"Now, it is time you find your sisters."

Protector.

Following my mother's instruction, I flew to a neighbouring island, where my sisters had been wreaking havoc of their own.

"Will they forgive me?" I had asked her before setting off.

"There is nothing to forgive," my mother replied firmly.

As she advised, I headed to the forest at the heart of the island. Once there, it took no time at all to locate my sisters, I just had to follow the unmistakable sound of their screeching cackles.

"Sisters!" I called out when I spotted them in a small clearing a little way ahead. They were lounging in a pool of cold sunlight and covered in dark, glistening blood. I knew immediately that the blood was not their own. At the sound of my voice they leapt to their feet with a shriek of pure delight, causing a rush of love and relief to swell inside my chest.

"Medusa, you look hideous!" Stheno barked out a laugh.

"Positively grotesque!" Euryale chimed in, snickering.

"You both look pretty awful yourselves." I couldn't help but smile as I hugged them tightly, unfazed by their bloody appearances. "I suppose we finally look related now."

"Isn't it fabulous?" Euryale gave a flamboyant twirl, her scales winking in the delicate morning light.

"You mean; you don't mind?"

"Are you kidding?" Stheno grinned. "Being hideous is *far* more fun than being beautiful." She was right about that.

"But, before...you were so upset." I turned to Euryale, still finding it difficult to meet her gaze.

"Oh, I was just being dramatic," she said breezily, rolling her dark eyes.

"Now we all finally fit in the family, eh?" Stheno gave us both a nudge.

"I love your snakes." Euryale stroked them gently. "They're wonderful."

Don't touch, they hissed at her, though I had come to realise only I could hear their whisperings. I willed them to settle down and they begrudgingly obeyed my silent command.

"Mother says you can turn men to stone just by *looking* at them – is it true?" I wasn't sure if I had imagined the touch of awe in Stheno's voice.

"Can you not do the same?"

"It seems that was another special gift to you from Athena." She gave a seemingly indifferent shrug, though I could definitely sense her jealousy now. It almost made me laugh – for the first time in our lives *they* were jealous of *me*.

Everyone is jealous of the powerful Medusa, the snakes chorused. They were constantly whispering things like this, endlessly stroking my ego. In hindsight, I hadn't realised how dangerous that could be.

"Well you better not get on the wrong side of me then." I smirked, but to my surprise my sisters looked genuinely uneasy. "I'm teasing, of course! Besides, it only seems to work on mortals."

"So, what did you think of mother?" Euryale grinned.

"She was very...persuasive." I found it difficult to encapsulate our encounter in a simple word.

"Persuasive?" Stheno cocked an eyebrow.

"She had me...*dispose* of a ship full of men." I could feel a sinister smile hinting at my lips as I spoke.

"You mean you took them all on by yourself?" Euryale gasped, awestruck.

"Well... I left a few alive," I replied with a chuckle, as a very unfamiliar feeling unfurled in my chest – I felt proud of myself.

You should be proud. Powerful Medusa.

My sisters then gushed about all the fun they had been having since I had disappeared. It seemed they were thoroughly enjoying their new bodies and the terror they could now inflict on the world. Stheno called it 'cleansing the land' which, in other words, meant they were flying around and disposing of those they deemed evil.

"It's mostly men," Euryale said.

"It's *all* men," Stheno corrected.

"I will gladly join the cause."

Before I continue, I just want to interrupt to say that I recognise my following actions were wrong. Now I have had an eternity to think and reflect, I realise that meeting violence with violence is never the answer, of course it isn't. All that does is let the infection fester and spread. It doesn't help anyone.

But let me tell you, I do not regret my actions either. You might think that heartless, but really, am I the one to blame here? I never wanted any of this. I was content with living a quiet and forgettable life as a priestess. If you ask me, it is the Fates' fault. They are the ones who intertwined this evil into my life, forcing me to become the villain in a story I never wanted to be a part of. They wanted a monster and so I gave them their damn monster. The blood is on their hands, not mine. The guilt is theirs to bear and yet...why do I still feel it weighing down upon me?

Our wrath spread like a disease.

We travelled across the land, leaving a trail of destruction in our wake. We infiltrated towns and cities, hunting out men who deserved to answer to our fury. Sometimes we caught them red-handed in their vile acts. Other times, we just acted on instinct, sensing the ones who deserved to be punished. I cannot even picture most of our victims anymore – it is all a haze of blind hatred and cold stone.

I remember that we had somewhat of a system, though. Euryale and Stheno would corner the man, mock and taunt him until he was quaking with terror and then I would emerge, the grand finale – capturing our victim in his last moment of pure, raw terror.

"We should put all our statues somewhere," Stheno said one day.

"Start a little collection," Euryale agreed.

"We could rank them, from best to worst kill."

"They are better left where they are," I told them. "Let the others see, let the fear spread."

It certainly did. Within just a few weeks, the news of our destruction had spread like wildfire; everyone was talking about the terrible Gorgon sisters. Within a month I had become the most famed monster in the land, just as Hermes had foretold. Soon we no longer even had to seek men out, they were coming to us. Everyone wanted to be the hero to slay the famous, deadly sisters, but of course none were successful in their task. We felt unstoppable. We felt like Gods.

You are better than the Gods.

Of course, the real Gods were untouchable. I would never be able to make Poseidon or Athena answer for their crimes; all

I could do was take my revenge elsewhere. So I funnelled my bitter hatred through acts I deemed as justice, using my curse to protect women from ever having to endure what I went through. With each victim I looked upon I imagined Poseidon's arrogant eyes staring back, turning slowly to cold, dead stone. I told myself I was righting the wrongs the Gods never would and I believed, in a perverse way, that I was finally living up to my name. *Protector*.

But in hindsight, I do not think 'protection' was the only reason for my violent actions.

Time takes a lot from you – beauty, memories, youth. But it can also give you many gifts as well, one of which is a sense of perspective. Now that I have had time to reflect on the damage I caused, I think I have realised what I was too numb to accept back then. I was not trying to destroy men; I was trying to destroy myself. I wanted to obliterate all memories of that helpless, beautiful, weak Medusa. If I could make the world my victim, then perhaps I could forget what it had felt like to be one myself. Perhaps I could finally, fully detach myself from my past.

But of course, it is never that simple is it? And no matter how many lives I ended, I could never change my own. My narrative had already been set and all I could do was fall helplessly into the future the Fates had decided for me.

You see, we are all the Fates' victims in the end.

The Boy.

You might wonder, did I enjoy it? Turning all those men to cold, lifeless stone. I try to tell myself I did not, because to enjoy murder would make me pure evil, would it not? But to be honest, some days I am not so sure. I cannot deny the thrill of being so deeply feared. I can assure you, it is far more rewarding to see a man's eyes fill with terror than ugly lust. Admittedly, I sometimes miss that feeling of power.

But power is a dangerous thing. Intoxicating and all-consuming. It is a type of poison that infects your whole being, rotting you from the inside out.

I should have realised that sooner.

I must confess that I told a lie just now. When I said I do not regret any of my actions, that was only partly true. I do not regret *most* of my actions. However, there is one victim who has haunted me since the day I took his life and I believe he will continue to for the rest of my eternity. If I could undo his death, I would do so in a heartbeat.

I do not even know his name.

"I want the first kill!" Stheno announced one day, as we approached our next target. We were heading towards a small fishing town settled right at the water's edge, where the mismatch of houses clung precariously to the land. There was no direct reason for us to target this settlement, its only crime was that it just so happened to fall into our direct line of vision as we hunted for our next victim.

We always attacked at nightfall, once the Goddess Nyx had wrapped her dark embrace around the world. It was safer, concealed by her darkness, but it was also the best time to sniff out our prey. You see, the night has a strange effect on men. It is as if the darkness allows them to peel away their decency, loosening their morals like you would loosen a tie at the end of a hard day's work. They *earned* this, they just needed to *blow off some steam.* Men would step out into the world and feel the night swell with possibilities, with all the things these respectable gentlemen would never *dream* of doing in the harsh light of day.

The town appeared fast asleep as we approached, the lights in every home were out. The only sound we could hear was the gentle lapping of the waves against the creaking boats, tied up in neat bobbing rows.

"How disappointing," Stheno muttered, as we strode through the empty gloom.

"Just wait," I breathed, feeling the snakes slithering excitedly over my skin. They always became agitated before a kill.

Hunt them down, Medusa.

Find them.

Kill them.

Over there, look.

"Up ahead." I nodded, clocking two shadows shuffling a little way ahead. As we drew closer we heard their voices splintering the peaceful quiet.

"Lykon, I have already told you that I am not interested unless you can pay." That was a female voice.

"Oh come on, don't be such a tease," the male voice slurred.

"Stop it, you're drunk. Just go home."

"Come on, you know you want to…"

"Go home to your family, Lykon."

"Come on…"

I nodded to my sisters and they immediately surged forwards, letting out a screech of excitable fury. I stood back, watching with a faint smile as the figures immediately broke apart. The woman ran off screaming, whilst my sisters surrounded the man, their blood curdling cackles bringing the cold, dead night to life.

The man fell to his knees, spluttering out the usual string of useless pleas. We had heard them all before. "Please, don't do this…please, I have a wife…a son… I am a good person…" His teary words fell flat and useless at my sisters' feet, as they circled round and round him, predators closing on their prey. "Zeus, please protect me! Please!"

"The Gods do not care about you," I hissed as I approached, "they do not care about any of us."

"Please." He reached out towards me, his body quaking with pitiful sobs.

"Look at me," I ordered.

"Oh Gods! Zeus protect me!"

"Look." I narrowed my deadly gaze, preparing myself for the final moment, feeling that familiar coldness cutting inside me. But, suddenly, my attention was caught by a rush of footsteps behind me.

"Father?"

I turned instinctively and was met with a different pair of eyes, softer, younger. The eyes of a child.

"Son!" The man rushed forward, but he only managed a few steps before my sisters knocked him to the ground. His body fell heavily, limp and lifeless.

"Well that was easy." Stheno's voice was behind me, flickering with sinister delight.

I could not respond. I could not take my eyes off the newly formed statue standing before me. A boy. A child. His face was frozen in a look of innocent fear, his mouth slightly open, revealing a missing front tooth. I had killed a child. As the realisation dawned, I felt guilt rising up inside me, threatening to spill over and consume me.

No, Medusa! Do not feel guilty.
Guilt is for the weak!
Think of what he would have turned into.
Think of what he would have become.
You have rid the world of another predator.
He deserved this. They all do.

I allowed the snakes' words to soothe me, because accepting their lies was far easier than facing the hideous truth. So I did what all cowards do and I buried that guilt deep down, locking it away alongside all the neglected grief I had left to fester inside me.

Let me just say, I do not blame you if you judge me for this, in fact, I encourage you to do so. This guilt is just something I have learnt to live with, along with all my other ugly scars. I have been haunted by that boy's face for so long, it is as if he has become my permanent companion down here in the beyond. I just wish I knew his name. I do not even know why; what difference would it make?

"He is just a boy," Euryale whispered as she appeared beside me, staring into the stony eyes of the dead child.

"Yes," I replied evenly. I could feel Euryale and Stheno's eyes on me as I walked away, without giving the boy a second glance.

Well done, Medusa.
Powerful Medusa.
Remember guilt is for the weak.
You are above that.
You are above everyone.

Snakes.

We did not mention the boy again. The snakes blocked him from my mind, along with all the other emotions they did not want me to feel. They had a real knack for blocking things out.

My snakes, my little 'gift' from Athena. It took me far too long to realise how toxic they really were.

They whispered endlessly in my ear and I grew weak to their suggestions, letting them pollute my mind. They fed my hatred, making sure I remained on my path of destruction. They constantly stroked my ego, reminding me how superior I was to everyone and everything, even my own sisters. In fact, it was one of their favourite pursuits, to regularly remind me how much better I was than Euryale and Stheno, how they would be nothing without me and how much of their success they owed to me... These lies clogged my mind, suffocating my own reasoning, until one day I made the terrible mistake of letting their words become my own.

We had been bathing in a nearby stream, a moment of precious peace before our next attack. Stheno and Euryale had been ruining the calm by disagreeing about something childish, I cannot even remember what it was now. I had been lying on the river bank, trying to ignore their rising voices. I was so quick to anger in those days; I could feel it constantly squirming beneath my skin, waiting to strike. The snakes slithered into my ear.

Make them shut up.
They are so useless.
And pathetic.
They hold you back, Medusa.
They are not good enough for powerful Medusa.
Tell them. Go on.

"Would you just SHUT UP?" I snapped and they fell immediately silent, surprised by the severity in my tone. I had been growing colder towards them in the past weeks, even I had noticed it, but I had never directly yelled at them.

"What's up with Medusa?" Stheno muttered to Euryale, loud enough to ensure I could hear.

"Beats me." Euryale shrugged, throwing me a filthy look.

They are insolent.
They should not talk to the powerful Medusa like that.
They should pay for their lack of respect.
Make them pay.

"What is *up* with me?" I rose and rounded on them. "I am tired of you two being a dead weight around my neck, that's what's *up with me.*" They both just stared at me, their expressions infuriatingly impassive.

Yes, Medusa! the snakes congratulated excitedly.
Let them have it.
Tell them they are worthless.
Tell them they are nothing without you.

"You would be nothing without me." The words slipped out in a hiss. I felt guilty as soon as I had said it, but guilt was a sign of vulnerability and I could not bear to show any weakness back then, even to my own sisters. So I smothered that guilt with blind and ugly anger.

"Is that what you think of us?" Euryale spoke quietly.

106

"I am tired of the pair of you," I responded, unable to look at the hurt in her eyes.

"Get off your power trip, Medusa." Stheno rolled her eyes dismissively.

"You dare talk to me like that?" I could feel my eyes glowing with fury, my entire body gripped by a sudden overwhelming bloodlust. I wanted to kill. I ached for that intoxicating feeling of total power, total ownership over a life. I was like an addict craving their poison.

"What's the matter with you, Medusa?" Euryale shook her head slowly.

"Perhaps we should just leave her alone, Euryale. We don't want to upset *Powerful Medusa*." Stheno's voice dripped with icy venom. Something must have flickered across my face as she spoke, because Stheno smiled coldly and continued. "Yes, we've heard you muttering to yourself like some lunatic... *Great Medusa, Powerful Medusa.*"

"You clearly think you are so much better than us now."

You are better than them.

"I am better than you," I retorted sharply. It was as if I had pressed a dagger into my chest and instead of just pulling it out, I was twisting it further and deeper inside. I do not know what was wrong with me, I just couldn't stop.

"Medusa, you are embarrassing yourself now." Stheno gave an empty laugh, folding her arms.

"Just admit it, Stheno, you cannot handle being the weaker sister," I sneered at her. "You hate being in my shadow, don't you? You are jealous."

"Jealous?" Stheno scoffed, turning to Euryale with an incredulous expression. Euryale remained quiet, watching us nervously.

"Yes, jealous," I repeated slowly. "You are jealous that I am the powerful one now."

"You are pathetic, Medusa. You always have been," Stheno spat. That touched a nerve and she knew it would.

"I am more powerful than you could ever dream of being!" The anger rushed from my body in a stumble of hateful words. "You two are nothing compared to me. You hear me? You are *nothing*!"

Well done, Medusa.

They deserve to know.

I thought Stheno would retaliate. I expected her to match my fury and hurl hateful words back in my face. But she didn't, she simply said nothing and that was the worst response of all.

"Come on, Euryale." She turned to our sister. "Let's go." Euryale gave me a tortured look before following after Stheno.

As I watched them leave I felt a tightness constrict inside my chest. Suddenly, I was unable to catch my breath. I doubled over, gasping for air as my vision swam. My whole body was trembling. I am quite sure I was having what you would call a panic attack, though of course I did not know it then.

Medusa, calm down.

Breathe, Medusa.

You are better off alone.

You do not need them, Medusa.

You have us.

We are all you need.

We will never betray you.

"You are right," I whispered raggedly, once I had managed to steady my breathing. "You are always right."

And so, once again, I allowed the snakes' voices to shield me from my guilt, drowning out the unbearable pain lurking inside me. I forced myself to believe their words, allowing them to numb me from reality, blocking my mind from the aching sense of loss that had opened up inside me. *Block it all out.* I could not bear to feel the pain, because I believed pain was weakness and I had promised myself I would never allow myself to be weak again. Never.

"I am better off without them," I told myself, pretending I believed it. "I do not need them."

Of course this was a lie. Of course I needed them. They were all I had left in the world. Who was I without my sisters? What was the point without them? I know that I could have gone after them, I could have tried to plead my case and earn back their love. But I did not believe I deserved their forgiveness. I felt I deserved to be hated, to be abandoned.

After losing my sisters, I lost all motivation. I felt myself slipping back into the familiar darkness, like submerging myself beneath murky waters. The snakes tried to pull me back from the abyss, but I was lost and listless. I had numbed myself to feeling and now I felt nothing at all.

I was empty.

But little did I know, I was quite the opposite.

Hard Feelings.

"Help! Please!" The man's cries echoed across the empty valley. He really shouldn't have been wandering out so far on his own, but I suppose it wasn't his fault that he had caught me in a particularly foul mood. It had been a week since my sisters had left me and I'd been walking listlessly across unfamiliar lands. I had started to feel sick and unsettled each morning, which only served to scratch at my already heated temper.

I spotted the man a way off – he was obliviously heading straight towards me. I had no motivation to attack him, but I knew if Euryale and Stheno had been here they would have planned a whole ambush, something that would have scared him senseless. I could almost hear their peals of laughter on the breeze and the thought made my chest ache. But my sisters were not here, I reminded myself coldly and I was not in the mood for such games. Instead, I just stood and watched as the man walked unsuspectingly towards his death.

"Medusa?" He recognised me as soon as he caught sight of me, of course he did, but even his helpless cries weren't a comfort to me anymore. The snakes rattled eagerly, urging me on.

Get him, Medusa.
Kill him.
Show him your power. Go on.
Do it.

Lacking any real enthusiasm, I turned my deadly gaze onto the man and watched as he let out a piercing wail, falling to his knees and raising his hands up to the sky in a melodramatic final pose. For a moment, he just stayed like that. He was motionless, but his flesh was still visibly soft and warm and very much alive. I glowered at him, incredulous. *How* could he still be alive? How was that possible? In all these months I had been attacking, I had never once made a mistake...

Then, to my surprise, the man started to laugh. It was a smooth, musical laugh, one I had heard once before in my life. My surprise immediately melted into irritation.

"Hermes." I nodded to him, my voice steady.

"So, we meet again." He rose to his feet, his human disguise peeling away as he shifted back into his godly form. I felt my skin prickle in his presence, but it no longer frightened me. I had endured the worst of the Gods' wrath and here I was, still standing, so why should I be intimidated by this little imp?

He is pathetic.

Not strong like you.

Nobody is like you.

"Yes," I silently agreed. It all made sense to me now. The Gods were powerful, but only in a superficial sense. Gifted at birth, life had handed them everything they ever wanted and everything else they simply took without repercussion. They were untouchable and that is what made them weak. You see, the Gods will forever be unaffected by the sufferings that strengthen the rest of us. They could never master the kind of power I possessed, of course not, because that power only comes from enduring, enduring the deepest pain and darkest moments of your life. The Gods had no idea of such concepts.

True strength only comes from suffering.

And that is why I was so damn powerful.

"That was a nice little act there." I stared directly at Hermes, chin slightly raised. I wanted to show I was no longer afraid of him. Admittedly though, it did feel strange to look a man in the eyes and have him stare straight back.

"I'm quite good at being a mortal," Hermes chuckled, his features brightened by that permanent mischievous grin hitched at the corner of his lips. "The trick is you just have to act really dumb."

"So what do you want?" I asked bluntly and a wisp of surprise caught somewhere in Hermes' eyes.

"Not going to offer me wine this time, I take it?" He winked, but I noticed that even he found it difficult to hold my gaze for too long. I started walking away from him, not bothering to turn to check if he was following. "Or do you only drink the blood of mortals now?" He fell into pace beside me.

"I prefer the hearts of men," I responded flatly and Hermes let out a high-pitched laugh.

"So how is it then, being a big scary monster?"

"Better than being a weak pathetic girl."

"See, I told you that you'd be famous."

"You didn't tell me the cost of it." Despite my words, my tone was emotionless.

"Hmm, yes, I suppose you're right…but I did *try* to warn you. It isn't *my* fault mortals are so useless at picking up clues, is it?" Hermes flashed me a conniving look. "Anyway, between you and me, I'm not a fan of Poseidon either… I mean, really, I don't know *why* Zeus lets him command the whole ocean when he can barely hold an interesting conversation. Trust me, he is the *last* person you want to be stuck next to at a banquet. All he talks about is himself." I stared blankly ahead, trying to remain

112

impassive at the mention of Poseidon's name. I assumed Hermes was just trying to provoke me with these trivial complaints, but I would not let him get under my skin so easily; to do so would be playing right into his hands.

"Why are you here again?" I asked with a sigh.

"You really aren't one for small talk, are you?" I noticed Hermes was hovering beside me now, his sandals whirring at his ankles, so fast you could barely see the wings at all. He floated in circles around me and I could feel my snakes writhing, embodying my irritation.

Let him have it.

Kill him.

He cannot mock the Great Medusa.

"He is a God," I told them silently, "don't be stupid."

"Tell me, how are your lovely snakes?" Hermes smirked, eyeing them curiously. "Make good pets, do they? Low maintenance? I suppose you don't have to take them for walks, at least…" One of the snakes nearest Hermes darted out, but he effortlessly dodged its attack, his smile unfaltering. "Short-tempered like you, I see."

"Only when provoked," I countered evenly.

"And how are they at conversation?" His question caught me off guard, causing my mask of impassivity to slip ever so slightly. But it was enough for Hermes to notice and his smile broadened as he realised he had finally struck a nerve.

"What do you mean?" I tried to keep my tone level. I had never told anyone about their voices, not even my sisters.

Do not tell him, Medusa.

Remember it is our secret.

He cannot know.

"The voices," Hermes said casually, "I am assuming they talk to you?" He stared directly into my eyes and for the briefest moment I considered lying, though I quickly realised that would be idiotic. Hermes would undoubtedly see right through me and lying would only show weakness.

"Yes, they do."

Medusa! No!

He must not know!

"I knew it!" Hermes' eyes sparked excitedly. "An interesting touch from Athena." He regarded my snakes with a keener interest, tapping his chin thoughtfully. "But obviously you know *why* she did that." It was not posed as a question, but Hermes must have known I did not know the answer. I felt the irritation itch at my skin, I did not want to ask what he meant, because I did not want to give him that power over me.

Ignore him, Medusa. He knows nothing.

You only need to listen to us.

"Why?" I sighed.

He knows nothing.

"Why what?" Hermes cocked his head to one side, wearing a face of patronising innocence. "Oh…you mean you *don't* know?" I held his gaze, refusing to ask again. "Well it's pretty obvious." He lowered himself softly onto the ground, a triumphant look sparking in his eyes. "I'm surprised you haven't realised already, if I'm honest."

"For Gods' sake, Hermes."

"Okay, okay!" He held up his hands in mock surrender. "The snakes are *obviously* there to drive you insane."

"Insane?" This was not what I had expected, though there seemed to be some logic to it…

Liar!

He is trying to weaken you, to drive us apart.

Do not listen to his lies, Medusa.

114

We are strongest together.

"They are telling you to not listen right now, aren't they?" Hermes' voice sounded muffled over the snakes' incessant hissing.

"Something like that," I responded levelly, trying to cut through the voices crowding my mind. I felt a headache begin to split at my temples. "So, you think Athena wanted to drive me insane?"

"I'm quite sure of it." Hermes nodded. "I mean, having voices constantly muttering in your ear – insanity is an inevitability, is it not?"

Liar! Liar!

"Well, how do I…stop it? How do I *not* go insane?" I hated asking for his advice, but I felt a surge of desperation grip me and the questions fell from my lips before I could stop myself.

"I suppose you just have to *not* listen." Hermes shrugged nonchalantly. "I mean; you've not gone mad yet – so that's something."

"Very helpful," I muttered.

We continued walking in silence for a little while, though it felt far from silent inside my mind – Hermes' words echoed on repeat, fighting against the ceaseless hissing: *He lies, he lies!* I barely had space for my own thoughts. My head throbbed with the chaotic cacophony of voices. Perhaps I already was insane.

"There is a reason I came," Hermes finally said.

"What is it?" I sighed. I wasn't entirely sure if I had the patience to take on any more of Hermes' meddling.

"I wanted to say: no hard feelings." Hermes locked eyes with me and I tried to find the hint of amusement lurking there, but to my surprise he looked serious, perhaps for the first time in his life.

"Why does nothing you say ever make sense?" I groaned. "Life would be so much easier if you just got to the bloody point."

Hermes snickered at this, his expression brightening once again.

"I like you Medusa." He caught me off guard with this. "That's why I want to say no hard feelings for what I'm going to have to do."

"And that is…?"

"I must aid the man who will come to kill you." His words were light, but there was a heaviness in his gaze which unsettled me. "It's the will of the Fates, my hands are tied with this one…"

"Many men have tried, I wouldn't worry." I tried to shrug off his look.

"Ah yes, but this one will succeed." Hermes tilted his head slightly, his golden ringlets falling over his sparkling blue eyes. Was he enjoying this? I honestly couldn't tell.

"Well, we'll see about that." My voice was surprisingly calm, as I felt a strange numbness settling over me. I didn't want to give him the satisfaction of my fear.

He lies again! We will never die!

We will never be defeated!

"It's a real shame," Hermes continued, with a dramatic sigh, "you know, with the baby and all."

"The what?" I shot him a deadly look – if he were mortal he would have been a lump of stone within seconds. If only.

"The baby… You must have realised by now, surely? I mean, you're even starting to show…" Again he wore that look of irritating fake innocence. He knew exactly what he was doing and he was loving it. "Have you thought of any names yet? 'Poseidon Junior' has a nice ring to it, don't you think?" His lips slowly curled into a malicious smile.

It was as if the world had been loosened. Everything around me began to tilt and slip away; even the snakes' voices were distant in my head. I thought I might collapse; I could not even sense the ground beneath me anymore. The only thing I could feel was the cold realisation shuddering throughout my body.

Pregnant.

As soon as Hermes had said it, it seemed so obvious. The sickness that had been churning away inside me, the swelling in my stomach, those unfamiliar twinges and spasms that had been pulsing through my body. Had I already known and just been ignoring it? Had I been lying to myself? Or had the snakes been drowning out the truth, blocking me from the reality, as they did with all my thoughts they deemed 'unwanted'?

Powerful Medusa.
We only did it to protect you.
You were not ready to know.
It was for the best.
The realisation would have made you weak.
It would have made you vulnerable.
We did it for you. Our Queen Medusa.

I closed my eyes, willing the world around me to settle back into place. I could not show this kind of weakness in front of Hermes. *Stop it.* I steadied myself against a nearby tree, feeling reassurance in the firmness of the rough bark beneath my trembling hands. A nausea crippled my stomach as the waves of understanding hit me one after the other, like a relentless storm battling against a weathered ship desperately trying to remain afloat.

It was *his* child.

It was a child of lust and violence. A child born from the darkest moment of my life. How could I bear that poison inside me? How could I ever love such a thing? Was there no end to my punishments?

"You look like you're going to throw up. Morning sickness?"

117

Hermes asked dryly. I tried to focus my gaze on him, I had almost forgotten he was still here.

"It's his child," I breathed, feeling the repulsive memories of him swarm my mind.

"I could get rid of it. If you wanted?" Hermes offered this as casually as if he were offering a cup of wine. "Just say the word…" He held out his open palm to me.

"No!" The word cut through me as I instinctively recoiled backwards, feeling a sudden overwhelming protectiveness. Looking back now, even in that initial stage of fear and confusion, I believe some part of me knew that I already loved the child growing inside me, regardless of who its father was. Yes, it was his child, but it was also mine. Mine to protect. *Mine.*

"No?" A knowing smile crept across Hermes' lips.

"I want the child to live." My voice sounded faint as a thought suddenly darkened my mind. "Will it live?"

"I don't know the specifics."

"Please, tell me." I hated begging, but I just had to know. Hermes regarded me slowly, as if weighing up the options inside his head.

"Some things are in our power and some are not." He looked at me pointedly, as if trying to convey some unspoken message. "That's all I can say…"

"But-"

"I've said what I came here to say, it's time for me to go now," he cut across me abruptly, his eyes bright and alert. "Goodbye, Medusa. I'll see you when all this is over." Before he left, he cast one more look at my stomach. "Maybe you could call him Hermes Junior? I'd be flattered, you know."

"How do you know it will be a boy?"

But he did not stay to answer. Instead, he kicked off into

the sky, his winged sandals humming away at his ankles. Within seconds he was blotted out by Helios' chariot, leaving me alone once more. But then again, I was not alone, was I? In fact, I would never be again. I placed my hands over my stomach, trying to feel the life stirring inside me.

"I will protect you," I murmured softly, "I promise."

Mother-To-Be.

The snakes did not like being ignored. But I had to will myself to shut them out. I hate to admit it, but Hermes' words had been the wake-up call I had sorely needed. I had been letting the snakes infect my mind for too long; they had driven me to endless violence, turned me against my sisters and even blinded me to my own pregnancy. Well, I had had enough of their poison and I could not bear the thought of giving Athena the satisfaction of driving me insane.

Do not ignore us, Medusa.

Let us in.

Let us be one.

You are weak without us.

After a while, their words turned bitter and cruel. Though this made them easier to ignore, as self-hatred was something I was well versed in.

You are weak.

Pathetic.

You are nothing without us.

Your child will die without us.

"Shall I cut off your heads and see what you have to say then?" I warned. That shut them up, for a while anyway. But, as time went on their voices gradually grew dimmer, gifting my mind with a newfound clarity. It was like a breath of fresh air, to be able to think my own, uninterrupted thoughts. I was not sure if I had silenced the snakes for good, or if I had just become better at blocking them out. Either way, they became an afterthought for me, as my mind was too preoccupied with the far more important matter at hand – my unborn child.

With each day that passed I felt my body changing. It was a wonderful, exhilarating feeling. And as the child grew, the world around me shrank – nothing else mattered anymore, he was my whole world now. Perhaps you are wondering, how could I love a child conceived by rape? To be honest, there is no real way to answer this question. I know this situation will be different for every victim who endures it, but for me I felt there was simply no alternative. I loved that child, whether I wanted to or not. He was mine and mine alone. I told myself he would be the one thing in my life I would do right by. I promised him.

Let me tell you, being pregnant is wonderful. But being pregnant when you are a wanted monster is not so picturesque. While I had forgotten about the world, it had certainly not forgotten about me. Men across the land were rallying together to try to hunt down the famous snake-haired Gorgon. They wanted my head as a trophy and the glory that would come with it, but all I wanted was to be left alone. Although I felt I couldn't be too bitter about this, considering I technically provoked them first. I had hurled my anger and hatred at the world, spreading misery in a vain attempt to stifle my own. I should have expected it to be thrown back in my face, shouldn't I? After all, violence only ever breeds more violence.

I used to not care that I was hunted. In fact, I welcomed the challenge. I wanted that reckless thrill. But now I had something to live for and with it came an overwhelming sense of vulnerability. I knew now I was not invincible, Hermes had made that clear enough. A man would come one day and he would kill me. But this did not worry me, in fact I had always somehow sensed my days would be numbered. What actually frightened me was the risk of my child never being born, of him dying with me. It was not his fault his mother was a monster and yet his life was threatened because of it. I remembered Hermes' words, *some things are in our power and some aren't.* I could accept my looming death, but I had to live long enough for my child to be born, I had to make that within my power. He had to live.

So, I did the only thing I could – I hid from the world. I flew to the furthest land, lost in the farthest sea, where I planned to wait out my pregnancy in quiet peace. Or so I had thought.

"Why are you hiding like a coward, Medusa?" My mother appeared on the island shortly after my arrival. Her voice was cold and rippling, her lips shrivelled in disgust. She did not even comment on my belly, which had now swollen considerably.

"I am protecting my child," I told her, placing an instinctive hand over my stomach.

"You stay hidden out here and the world will forget about you," my mother warned, drawing closer. She smelt of salt and rotten fish. "Is that what you want, to be forgotten?"

No, we want to be remembered! I could faintly hear the snakes, still there, still persisting.

"I do not care anymore." I shrugged her off, walking past her up the shore. "I have something more important to focus on now."

"So, you would throw away your infamy for a child of rape?" my mother sneered, her eyes dark slits. Her words made me stop in my tracks; I felt the familiar anger rising inside me. "You would throw away your chance of being remembered throughout history?"

"Is it my fame you are worried about, or your own?" I countered, turning to face her. She opened her mouth to respond but I didn't give her the chance. "Don't lie mother, all you really care about is yourself. You are terrified of being forgotten, aren't you? You force your children to do hideous things, so you can leech off their infamy. It's pathetic."

"Do not dare talk to me like that, child," she spat. Behind her the sea began to grow restless, the waves rushing to shore and crashing around our ankles. "You will not throw this opportunity away, Medusa."

"I don't want to play your games anymore."

"You would disobey your own mother?" Another surge of waves swelled around us, angry and urgent. The water was up to our thighs now and I had to fight to keep my footing.

"Yes." I gave a humourless laugh. "Why wouldn't I? What have you ever done for me? You only ever loved me when you knew you could use me for your own fame."

"You are wrong about that." My mother took a step closer. "I never loved you." Her words were like cold glass cutting into my skin. But I forced myself to remain impassive, she did not deserve the pleasure of hurting me. "Nobody will ever love you, Medusa. You will die unloved and unwanted...but, you could still be *feared*, still be remembered, still be powerful in death." The familiar voices stirred again.

Powerful...

Feared...

Remembered...

"Stop it!" I was shouting now. "You are poison, that's all you are!"

"I had such hopes for you, Medusa. You had come so far..."

"Disown me then, abandon me, do what you want, I don't

care anymore. Just *leave me alone*." I began to walk away, wading through the swell of angry waves, but I was forced to stop when I heard her voice crawling eerily across the breeze.

"If you will not bring your destruction to them, then I will bring them to you." I turned to see a sinister smile creep across her cold face, her eyes narrowing. "This place isn't as well hidden as you think."

"Please, don't…my child…"

"It's for your own good." My mother was walking back into the ocean now, the frothing waves receding with her. "You will be famous, my child. You will be remembered. I will make sure of it."

"Mother, please, I beg you-"

But she was already gone, swallowed up by the dark ocean.

That would be the last time I ever saw my mother.

Hunted.

The location of the infamous 'Lair of Medusa' has been lost over time. Many have argued over its whereabouts and I will admit I have enjoyed a few good laughs hearing the groundless claims shouted across history. I could tell you now and eradicate the mystery, if I wanted to. But what would be the point? What good would it do, letting modernity know where Medusa spent her final days? I shudder at the thought of those inexperienced and overpriced tour guides ushering around flocks of tourists, reinforcing all those infuriating lies.

"Here is where the evil monster was slain…"

"…punished for luring Poseidon to her bed…"

"…and this is where the heroic Perseus saved the day…"

No, I will not be telling you the whereabouts. Now that the 'Lair of Medusa' is finally a mystery, I feel it should stay that way. I just wish it could have been kept a secret whilst I was still alive… but my dear mother made sure that was not the case.

It did not take long for them to find me.

I still remember feeling the anger and dread clotting inside me, when I saw that first ship approaching. It was just a small, dark stain on the horizon, but I knew what it meant: my mother had been true to her word and my child was no longer safe.

I stayed and watched as the ship prowled closer, the bow piercing through the folds of morning mist. As I gazed out across the hazy ocean, I decided then and there that I would not die today. I would not let these men kill me. This resolution hardened inside me, transforming my fear into a cold calm.

"Come on then," I muttered bitterly, "come to your death."

Powerful Medusa.

Great Medusa.

We have missed you.

As the boat drew closer, I finally turned and headed up the island. I did not want to be caught out in the open, it was too dangerous, I could be easily surrounded and stabbed in the back by some careless coward. If I were to dispose of these men quickly and safely, I would have to be smart about it. Fortunately, I knew of the perfect place. There was a cave near the heart of the island, deep and cavernous. There I could wait in the inky shadows, concealed until that final moment when the men would stumble foolishly to their deaths.

Come and get us…

As I waited in the shadows, I felt my child stirring inside me. Perhaps he sensed the danger we were in, because he began to kick restlessly, causing me to double over.

"Please, stop. It's okay little one," I cooed into the blanket of darkness, "we'll be okay, I promise."

Suddenly a great clamour echoed from the mouth of cave. The men were unsheathing their swords, preparing for a battle they would never have. From the sound of their chaotic argument, I guessed there must have been over a dozen of them.

"I'm going first."

"No, I am!"

"Hold on, I'm the one who's going to kill the bitch."

"No, no, I'm the one with the best aim."

"Oh come off it, I'm the strongest."

126

"You're also the stupidest."

"Shut up all of you, or she will hear us!"

"Are you scared?"

"Of course not. Don't be foolish. We just want to make sure she doesn't hear us first."

"That's a good point."

I rolled my eyes as they continued arguing in loud whispers, their clumsy footfalls growing closer. Surely my killer was not amongst this mob of idiots? If I were destined to die, could it at least be at the hands of a man with a functioning brain?

I steeled myself as they drew nearer, preparing to do something I knew would be foolish – but I felt it was at least worth a shot.

"Men!" I called out, my voice resonating powerfully off the cave walls, bringing the sinister darkness to life. They immediately fell silent, I could see the light from their torches just creeping around the corner – they were close, but they could not see me yet. "I know you have come here to slay me...but listen, I do *not* want to kill you. I do not want any bloodshed on my shores. I implore you to leave this island, live your lives and tell the world that Medusa's reign is no more."

"What is she on about?"

"She says she doesn't want to fight."

"Bollocks!"

"She's trying to trick us."

"I think she's just round here!"

"Come on! Me first!"

They surged forwards, a crash of bodies and weapons fighting against one another to be the first to reach me. In the end, it did not matter who got there first – within seconds they were nothing more than lifeless statues. As soon as their torches illuminated my deathly glare it was all over for them, they never even stood a chance. Afterwards, I stared out across their cold stone faces, that familiar sense of power buzzing through my veins. Some of them had not even had time to raise their weapons.

"See," I whispered, "I told you we would be okay."

As time passed, my empty 'lair' soon grew crowded, populated by lifeless bodies imprisoned in their final moments of defeat. In the gloom of the cave they almost appeared like frozen ghosts. I wonder if they are still there now, haunting those endless tunnels.

"Stheno and Euryale would have loved this," I murmured as I wandered amongst the statues, like a queen amongst her subjects. "They're your aunties. I hope you'll get to meet them one day..."

Despite my endless victories, I was still permanently gripped by fear. I spent my days intently watching the horizon, readying myself for another battle and wondering each time if it would be my last. I could not sleep, could not even rest my eyes for a single moment. My body ached from the relentless, exhausting tension. The snakes even managed to wriggle their way back in through the channels of my anxiety.

Was that a noise?

Is that a ship we see, there on the horizon. Right there!

We definitely heard something behind you, didn't you?

Are those shadows moving?

You might wonder why I didn't just leave and flee to a new, unknown island. But it would have been futile. My mother would have always found me and so the men would have always come. Wherever I was, I would never be safe.

But, after a time, my unwanted visitors became fewer and further between. I assumed that, as nobody had ever returned from their quests, people had begun to finally abandon their hope of claiming the head of the famous Medusa. At first, I did not dare trust the quiet, in fact it only put me more on edge. But as the weeks rolled by uninterrupted, I began to allow myself the dangerous gift of hope. My baby would be born; he would be okay. He would know his mother, he would be loved and happy. I even began to fool myself into thinking Hermes had been lying. He was a trickster after all, wasn't he? So how could I trust anything he said? Perhaps this was all part of his sick game and he had just wanted to get a kick out of scaring me.

Each morning I told myself everything would be okay, like a prayer and each time Helios finished his journey across another peaceful day, I began to believe it more and more.

"I cannot wait to meet you," I said to my dome-like stomach, smiling as I felt my boy kicking excitably in response.

It pains me now to think how hopeful I had let myself become, how I had actually *believed* I could live happily ever after... After everything I had been through, I was still so naïve. Had I not learnt anything? I guess some things never change.

Hope is a dangerous thing.

Warning.

It had been a drizzly, grey morning when I spotted the two winged figures down by the shore. I had been on my own for so long now, I thought perhaps I might have been dreaming. But as I heard the familiar voices carrying across the damp breeze, I felt a wide smile break across my face.

"This doesn't look like the right island."

"It is, I'm telling you."

"We definitely took a wrong turn back there."

"We didn't, she's here, I'm sure of it!"

"Euryale, you're terrible at directions, why did I let you lead…"

"Stheno, look!"

I was waddling awkwardly across the stony beach, moving towards them as fast as my swollen body would allow. I felt the relief blossom in my chest as they rushed towards me, their scaled and hideous bodies embracing my own.

"I've missed you both so much." Hot tears spilled down my cheeks, but I did not fight them, I was not afraid of showing this kind of vulnerability anymore – I knew I was stronger than that.

I clung to my sisters desperately, not wanting to let them go ever again. I had not realised how deeply I had needed them here. We stayed entangled in one another's arms for a little while, the emotional moment blanketed by the light rain drizzling around us.

"Well, you got fat," Stheno teased, when she finally drew back.

"You are ginormous!" Euryale gawped, her eyes then travelled up to my head. "Are your snakes sleeping? I have never seen them so still."

"I try to keep them quiet these days." My smile slightly faltered as I spoke. "Shall we get out of this rain?"

"So, is this your infamous secret lair?" Stheno grinned once we had reached the cave.

"Something like that."

I began coaxing a fire to life and couldn't help but smile at the sound of my sisters' shrieks of laughter resonating off the cave walls. They were busy exploring the various tunnels, finding great delight in my 'impressive' collection of victims.

"You've been quite busy." Stheno raised an eyebrow as she sat down beside the fire.

"Mother will be pleased," I muttered.

A quiet settled around us, punctuated only by the lazy crackling of the fire. I felt that familiar guilt pressing into my chest, as feeble apologies clogged in my throat. How could I put my shame into words? I had been so cruel to my sisters, after everything they had done for me, after what they had sacrificed for me. I knew I did not deserve them.

"I'm so glad you are here..." I began, my voice wavering slightly, "I...just mean...I wanted to say...that I'm..."

"It's okay." Stheno held my gaze across the fire, my unspoken apology hanging heavily between us. To my relief, she smiled.

"We missed you too!" Euryale chimed, grabbing my hand. I smiled back at them, allowing the relief to slightly ease the guilt wedged in my chest.

"How did you find me anyway?"

"Mother told us where you were."

"Seems she's telling everyone." I rolled my eyes.

"Well, she wouldn't tell us at first... She said something about wanting to teach you a lesson." Stheno tilted her head quizzically.

"We would have come sooner if we could!" Euryale said fervently, squeezing my hand tighter.

"Well you're here now and that's all that matters." I smiled at them, but felt it fade from my lips as I saw their expressions darken. "What is it?" They shared a sombre look, their features contorted by the dancing shadows. I could feel a familiar fear knotting inside me.

"We have come to warn you, Medusa," Stheno spoke first, looking reluctant. "There's a man, a hero, on his way here...to kill you."

"Many have already tried," I countered coolly, trying to shrug off the tension that had built around us. "You've seen for yourself, I've got quite the collection-"

"He's being aided by the Gods," Euryale cut across me, her voice cracking slightly as the emotion seeped through. "They're saying it's the will of the Fates."

The Fates. Of course. My old friends.

"We've heard Athena gave him a shield of some sort..."

Ah, and Athena too... I should have known she would be involved. Perhaps she was annoyed I hadn't gone entirely insane yet, so now she wanted a more permanent solution for me.

"And Hermes."

"Hermes?" His words suddenly awoke inside my head: *it's no hard feelings... I must aid the man who will come to kill you...* So, he had been telling the truth after all. I felt the realisation settle heavily over me. I was going to die.

132

"Apparently he gifted him a sword." Stheno's words curled with hatred.

"And winged sandals, like Hermes' own… It's basically cheating!" Euryale let out a childish whine.

"How do you know all this?" My voice was surprisingly calm.

"Mother told us. She heard word from the other Gods." Stheno's expression was stiff, I think perhaps she was trying to hold back tears.

A silence followed as I mulled over their words, staring into the heart of the spluttering fire. My mind was surprisingly clear, I had half expected the snakes to take advantage of this moment of weakness, but I was only dimly aware of them stirring at my temples, I couldn't even hear them hissing anymore.

"Do you know when he will be here?" I stared at my sisters, but even Stheno found it hard to meet my gaze now. "Well?"

"Tomorrow." Stheno's voice was just a ragged whisper, she turned her face into the shadows.

"We should have come sooner." Euryale was openly crying now, gripping my arm desperately as the tears streamed down her scaly cheeks. "We'll stay; we'll fight with you Medusa!"

"No, no, listen to me. Listen." My voice was suddenly firm. "You have to go, both of you."

"No-"

"Yes. You must." I gripped both their hands, gazing at each sister in turn. "I've put you both in enough danger already… You know as well as I do that if this is the will of the Fates then there is nothing we can do." Euryale let out a hiccupping sob. "This is my destiny and you must let me face it alone. Please."

"We are not leaving you, no matter what the Fates have planned." The firelight gleamed in Stheno's dark eyes, causing her unshed tears to sparkle.

133

"You have to. Listen, I need you both to stay safe because when the time comes, I need someone to look after my child." I placed their hands on my stomach, letting a quiet moment pass as we all felt him stirring inside me. My sisters stared at my belly in mournful wonder. "I need you to be there for him when I cannot be."

"But…how will he…?"

"I will make sure of it, no matter what." My voice caught in my throat ever so slightly. "He will be born; I promise you that."

"He will." Euryale managed a tear-streaked smile.

"He will." Stheno nodded firmly. "And we will be there for him. Always."

"Always."

Their words settled round the fire, like an oath being sworn. What did I ever do to deserve such wonderful sisters? I felt the emotion threatening to spill as it slowly seeped between the cracks forming inside me. But I knew I couldn't let it out, not yet. I had to stay strong, I had to hold it together. Just for a little while longer. My child's life depended on it.

"So," I tried to muster up a casual tone, in an attempt to break the heavy silence that had settled around us, "do you know the name of this so-called hero?"

"Perseus. His name is Perseus."

Perseus.

I am going to take a moment now to tell you a little about Perseus, because I think it is important you know some background to the man who ultimately ended my life. Let me just start by saying that everything I am telling you here I was told by Perseus himself and so I will try to stay as true to his own words as possible.

Firstly, it might surprise you to know that Perseus was a child of rape.

I have heard fanciful retellings of this myth, where Zeus supposedly transformed himself into golden rain and seeped into the skin of Perseus' mother, Danaë. It makes it sound so innocent, almost whimsical, doesn't it? But Perseus assured me that this was not the case. He spared me the full details, but I could tell enough from the disturbed darkness in his eyes.

So, Zeus forced himself on Danaë and from that violent lust Perseus was born. Though Danaë was not just a victim of Zeus, but also of her own father, Acrisius. Acrisius was king of Argos and a man riddled with paranoia and hate. He had Danaë locked up in a tower so he could do with her what he wanted and it was to his utter outrage that he had discovered she was impregnated by another. Fuelled by his poisonous rage, Acrisius threw his daughter and grandson into a chest and cast them out into the ocean to die. Some say Acrisius' violent actions were motivated by the Fates, who had foretold the king would die by the hands of his grandson. Though Perseus had told me that he believed Acrisius was simply driven by his fury over someone else touching what he believed to be 'his', even the King of the Gods.

Contrary to Acrisius' plan, Perseus and his mother did not die that day. Instead, they washed up on the island of Seriphos, where Danaë raised Perseus in peaceful solitude, finally free of her abusers. On Seriphos, Perseus had a humble upbringing. He and his mother made do with what they had, grateful enough just to have one another. Perseus adored his mother above all else, you could tell from the way he spoke about her with such loving respect. He idolised the woman.

Being the child of Zeus, Perseus grew with divinity firing in his veins. As time passed, he began to notice he could run faster than the other children, lift heavier, climb higher, his energy seemingly endless. But, instead of using his skills to seek out glory, as so many others did, Perseus instead found pleasure in simply helping those in his community. He told me this as if it were an obvious decision, but little did he realise how unique his selflessness made him.

Sadly, Danaë's suffering at the hands of men was not entirely over. Her beauty had attracted the unwanted attention of Polydectes, the King of Seriphos. Perseus was fully grown now and he was not ignorant of Polydectes' advances. He knew of his mother's dark past; she had hidden nothing from him and his respect for her only grew after understanding what she had endured. Perseus had vowed to protect his mother from ever experiencing such horrors again. So, Perseus stood in Polydectes' way at every possible turn, shielding his mother from the king's slimy grasp. But Polydectes, like so many other men, would not take no for an answer. He was the king and he would have what he wanted.

But, if Polydectes were ever to succeed in claiming Danaë, he knew he would need to get rid of her son for good. He spent many nights pacing in his palace, trying to conjure up a plan that would dispose of Perseus without getting any blood on his hands or scaring off Danaë. One day, he heard gossip of the famous snake-haired Gorgon and how no man who had faced the monster had ever lived to tell the tale. A dark plan immediately hatched in his mind.

"Perseus!" Polydectes came to the young man one day. Perseus was only half Polydectes' age and yet already he was taller and bigger than Polydectes had ever been.

"Can I help you?" Perseus was busy chopping wood and did not even bother to look up from his task. You might think his behaviour insolent, but to Perseus respect was something that had to be earned, not claimed by titles and wealth. "If it is my mother you are after, she is busy right now, so you should come back another time."

"I'm actually here for you, my boy," Polydectes said, his voice smooth and oily.

"I see." Perseus effortlessly swung the axe down onto another block of wood, splitting it perfectly.

"Well, Perseus." Polydectes had to awkwardly side step to avoid another explosion of splinters. "I know it is no secret that I am fond of your mother and wish to marry her." Perseus did not respond, he just made an indistinct noise at the back of his throat. "And you have also made it abundantly clear that you do not want that to happen."

"My mother does not want that to happen," Perseus said flatly.

"Well, whatever the case may be..." Polydectes waved off his words dismissively, to which Perseus rolled his eyes. "I have a deal to strike with you."

"A deal?"

"Yes, yes." Polydectes worked an amicable smile onto his pink, fleshy face. "Have you heard of the snake-haired Gorgon monster?"

"Medusa? Yes, of course. Everyone has."

"Well, my boy." Polydectes licked his lips. "If you bring me her head, I will leave your mother alone for good. I swear my life on it."

"Her head?" Perseus leant against his axe. "Why?"

"Why, she's the most infamous monster of our generation, my boy! That's why! A head like that on my mantelpiece will make me the most feared king in all the land." Perseus paused for a moment, a small frown gathering between his eyebrows.

"And that's the price for you to leave my mother alone?"

"Yes, yes, I promise! In fact, I will ensure that no man ever bothers her again." Polydectes sounded breathless now, but his eagerness only served to unsettle Perseus further.

"And what if I refuse?"

"Well, my boy." Polydectes flicked an invisible speck of dust from his immaculate robes. "If we cannot come to an agreement, then perhaps I will have to make some other arrangements for you and your mother." Perseus saw a darkness glint in Polydectes' eyes, his unspoken threat hanging between them.

"The Gorgon's head. That's all you want?"

"Yes, that is all."

"And then you will leave my mother alone?"

"You have my word, my boy."

"Fine." Perseus threw out his hand to Polydectes. "I'll do it."

"Excellent." Polydectes closed his hand around Perseus', a menacing smile hinting at his lips. In his mind, he had just sentenced Perseus to death.

Of course, Danaë had been less than happy about this arrangement. She knew as well as Polydectes did that no man had returned from this quest alive. But Perseus' mind was resolute; this was the only way to ensure his mother's safety and nothing was more important to him than that.

"Please, don't go." She wept silently into her son's arms.

"I'll be fine, it'll be easy," Perseus teased with a mischievous grin, but Danaë shook her head furiously, in no mood for games.

"Let's just leave, go somewhere else, get away from that hideous man…"

"Mother." Perseus cradled her head in his hands, tipping her face up to meet his. "Seriphos is our home, we are not leaving."

"I cannot lose you." Her words caught in her throat. "You're all I have."

"You won't."

"But–"

"Mother. You won't." He kissed the top of her head, tears glistening in his own eyes. He hated more than anything to see his mother upset, but he knew this had to be done and her tears could not sway him this time.

And so, at the break of day he set off on his quest to face the famous snake-haired Gorgon. To face his destiny. To face me.

But, for all his confidence, Perseus still had the slight problem of not knowing where he was heading. Of course, he had heard all about the terrible monster Medusa, but tracking me down proved to be a whole new and unexpected challenge. Perseus began by pursuing wisps of rumours, but each trail eventually went cold, leaving Perseus feeling like a dog endlessly chasing its own tail, never getting closer to his goal. Whereas once the world had actively sought me out, it seemed now the terrible 'wrath of Medusa' had scared people into silence. Wherever Perseus turned, he was met with nervous glances and awkward pauses; most people would not dare share even a scrap of information. It seemed many thought it a bad omen just to utter my name.

Despite these dead ends, Perseus remained determined and decided to turn to the Gods for guidance. Perseus travelled to Delphi to speak with the renowned Oracle, a priestess supposedly blessed with divine insight. Many men have bowed before the Delphic Oracle to hear her esteemed prophecies, including Perseus' own grandfather. However, for the hopeful Perseus, the Oracle's words had been brief and frustratingly vague.

"Your answers will find you," she spoke in a breathless whisper, her eyes glazed as she tilted precariously atop her tripod.

"How? How will they find me?" Perseus pressed, but he was already being ushered away by a shrewd looking priest announcing curtly that his time was up.

Now Perseus felt the dangerous weight of defeat hanging over him. He had spent the last of his money getting to Delphi and had nothing left but the Oracle's ambiguous advice turning over in his mind. What was he to do now? The thought of admitting defeat was unbearable to Perseus, how could he ever look his mother in the eye knowing he had failed her?

Perhaps, if Perseus had been an ordinary man, his quest would have ended there, unsatisfying and unsuccessful. But needless to say, Perseus was far from ordinary. The son of Zeus and chosen by the Fates themselves – of course Perseus would not fail his mission, though he did not know it then.

"This seat taken?"

Perseus had been sitting alone in the farthest corner of a tavern. It was a dingy, depressing place that stank of sweat and old meat. But Perseus did not care, he had just needed a place to quietly think. He was so submerged in his thoughts that he barely noticed the strange figure suddenly loom over him. Knocked into consciousness by this question, Perseus politely motioned to the seat before him, without really registering the stranger.

"It is a pleasure to finally meet you, Perseus." These words caught his attention, pulling his focus away from his internal frustrations. Perseus looked up and a sharp jolt knocked the air straight from his lungs – he was sitting across from a God.

"Hermes?" he breathed incredulously, looking around to see if anyone else had noticed an Olympian in their midst.

"They only see what I want them to see," Hermes chuckled, casting a conceited gaze across the oblivious, drunken crowd. There seemed to be some altercation near the doorway, two drunken men were shouting vulgarities at one another and threatening violence, though it seemed their only real fight was in trying to stand upright. One staggered into another man, drawing him and his companions into the raucous argument. Hermes watched the men with delighted amusement, whilst Perseus kept his eyes on the God, stunned into complete silence. It seemed utterly surreal, to see an Olympian sitting in this grimy little tavern, looking so absurdly out of place it was almost comical.

Eventually, Hermes drew his attention back to Perseus and said, "Vague, isn't she?" At Perseus' blank expression he added with a slight incline of his head, "The Oracle."

"Oh, yes." Perseus could barely curb the disappointment from his voice. "I just... I cannot make sense of her words."

"I wouldn't worry about it." A smirk tugged at one corner of Hermes' lips, his attention shifting back to the drunken fight as fists began to fly. "It's largely rubbish, the stuff she comes out with anyway. Though don't tell anyone I said that."

"It is?" Perseus whispered incredulously, leaning forward.

"So what's your plan, then? For killing Medusa?" Hermes pressed on, propping his elbows onto the table and resting his chin on his interlaced fingers. "I mean; you won't be able to kill her just with those devilish good looks of yours," he added with a wink.

"Um…well, firstly I just need to find where the monster lives… That's proving a little more difficult than I expected." Perseus could not understand the mischievous gleam in Hermes' eyes. Was he secretly laughing at him? What was the God's motive here?

"And then what?"

"Well, then I will behead the monster."

"With what?"

"With my sword…"

"With *that* thing? Oh, Perseus, no, no, no," Hermes drew back, tutting loudly and looking around as if the oblivious crowd would agree. "That will shatter into a million pieces before it gives Medusa so much as a scratch."

"Oh." Perseus glanced at his sword, deflated.

"And what about her deadly gaze? You know about that don't you?"

"Well, yes, I was thinking…"

"And her two sisters, have you thought about them at all?"

"Well, I…"

"And how about transporting her head afterwards? You do know her powers will still be deadly even after she is beheaded, right?"

"Well…no, I didn't…"

"Perseus, Perseus, Perseus," Hermes sighed, suddenly appearing right beside him with a pop of light. The God draped a long arm around Perseus' shoulders and gave him a gentle shake. "I understand you are clueless and afraid…"

"I never said-"

"But," Hermes cut over him smoothly, "never fear, because *I* am here to help you. You follow my guidance and you will find Medusa in no time at all."

"Th-thank you…" seemed the only adequate response Perseus could think of.

"Oh, and when you do find her, say hello from me will you?" There was a dark glint in Hermes' eyes. "She's an old friend."

When Perseus told me all about his adventures with Hermes, I could not help but laugh at his exasperated tone – it seemed I was not the only one who found the Trickster God infuriating. Though for all his irritating habits, Hermes had been helping him after all, so Perseus had to just nod and smile as he followed after the God like a helpless puppy.

Hermes firstly led Perseus to the Graeae, Grey Sisters. Three ancient hags who dwelled in the darkest depths of the Earth, closer to the realm of the dead than the living, so they say. These crones were technically my siblings, though I have not and will never meet them. Like so many of my relatives, they are nothing more than strangers to me.

"They know where to find Medusa," Hermes told Perseus as they approached the jagged, gaping mouth of the sisters' cave.

"But I thought you already knew where she is?"

"Of course I do," Hermes scoffed, "but where would the fun be if I gave you all the answers? Now, off you go… Enjoy!"

Perseus described the Grey Sisters as 'animated corpses', he said their eerily skeletal bodies were so withered and decrepit he wondered how they had enough breath in their lungs to exist, let alone speak.

"What do you want?" they had hissed at Perseus when he appeared, holding out the single blood-shot eye they famously shared between them.

"I seek the whereabouts of the Gorgon Medusa."

"Ah, yes, sister Medusa," they laughed scornfully. "Mother has told us all about her."

"Please, can you tell me where I can find her?"

"Why would we help you?" one spat.

"What would be in it for us?" the other added.

"I am sure we can come to an arrangement," Perseus replied. "What can I offer you in return?"

"How about your eyes?"

"Yes, yes, your eyes!"

"We could do with a matching pair." They began to cackle, licking their thin lips eagerly and revealing their pallid, toothless gums.

"I'm afraid I need my eyes, ladies," Perseus replied gently, his hand hovering over the hilt of his sword. "Is there anything else I can offer you?"

"Your teeth?"

"Your teeth would be lovely!"

"We could use some strong teeth."

"Unfortunately, I need those as well." Perseus tensed as the Grey Sisters began to inch forwards, their crooked fingers groping out towards him.

"What about just the one eye?"

"Or a handful of teeth?"

"That is the only way we will give you what you seek," the

shortest snarled and Perseus considered these words as the sisters closed in around him.

"Well, I am afraid my eyes and teeth are no good," he told them with an apologetic sigh.

"What?"

"No good?"

"How can that be?"

"I was born with terrible eye sight and rotten teeth." Perseus shook his head dramatically. "They have caused me endless trouble; I assure you ladies you wouldn't want them."

"Terrible?"

"Rotten?"

"He lies, he must lie!"

"By all means, take a look for yourself." Perseus then leant forward, fluttering his eyelashes and bearing his perfect teeth.

"Look sister, look!"

"Tell us what you see!"

"Move out my way!" The tallest bustled her sisters aside, the eyeball darting wildly in her hand as she scrutinised the hero. The foul stench of decay curled inside Perseus' nostrils as she leaned in closer and he could even see the thin veins pulsing beneath her wrinkled skin.

In a flash, Perseus reached out and snatched the eyeball from the woman's knotted fingers. The sisters let out a furious, blood-curdling screech and advanced on Perseus with surprising nimbleness.

"Wait, wait!" Perseus instructed them, gripping the eye tightly and holding his fist aloft. "If you take a step closer I will destroy it."

"You wretched beast!"

"You will pay for this!"

"I am sorry, I truly am." Perseus had to shout to cut over their wailing. "I do not wish to harm you. I just need to know the whereabouts of Medusa. If you tell me I will return your eye, unharmed. You have my word."

"Who are you?" one of the sisters sneered at him.

"Are you the one our mother speaks of?" the other asked.

"Are you Perseus?" the third interjected.

"I am."

"Then Gods help her."

After the Grey Sisters confirmed my location, Hermes equipped Perseus with everything he would need in order to kill me. It is laughable really, how my head was practically served up to Perseus on a silver platter. I never stood a chance, did I?

"Those suit you," Hermes marvelled as Perseus struggled into a pair of winged sandals, which perfectly matched his own. "Though I imagine you could pull off anything."

"They're...a bit...feisty..." Perseus huffed as the wings battled defiantly against him.

"Oh, that's standard, you just have to break them in," Hermes chuckled, watching Perseus grapple with the sandals without bothering to offer any help. Once Perseus finally managed to wrestle them on, Hermes cracked a broad smile. "Fabulous! Now, give me your best 'hero pose'."

"Um." Perseus hesitated. "Like this?" He awkwardly shifted his stance, raising his new glittering sword above his head, another of his gifts from the God.

"Now give the sword a swipe!" Hermes instructed, clapping his hands like an excitable child. Perseus obeyed, feeling the divine weapon buzz beneath his fingertips as he let it slice effortlessly through the air. "Perfect! Perfect! But..." He tilted his head to one side, scrutinising Perseus with slightly pursed lips. "Hmm...now you are just missing one thing..."

"Hermes." A voice resonated around them, cold and commanding.

"Sister Athena, impeccable timing as always!" Hermes called out and Perseus watched incredulously as the two Olympians greeted one another. He had only just grown used to Hermes' divine company and now here was Athena herself towering before him. He tried to hold his composure.

"Perseus." She nodded towards him, the plume of her helmet bristling. "You seek to kill the monster Medusa, yes?"

"I do, Wise Goddess." He bowed his head low, trying to keep his voice level.

"Good." As Athena drew closer, something materialised in her hands. "This is the final component you will need for your victory." Perseus stared in awe at the shield glittering brilliantly between them. He reached out to touch it, feeling a spark pulse through his fingertips.

"How can I ever thank you, Goddess?"

"Just make sure she dies." Athena smiled coldly.

"I will not disappoint you."

The Deal.

So now that you know a little more about Perseus, let me go back to that cold morning of his arrival, when I stood at the mouth of the cave, waiting for my killer. I'm sure a lot of you *think* you know this next part of the story, when the great, heroic Perseus snuck up on the sleeping monster, effortlessly cutting her head off and leaving the island victorious. Well, that is the version that history wants you to remember, a simple tale of good vs evil, of hero vs villain – an easy story to tell. But the truth isn't always so black and white, is it?

The rain had eased overnight, leaving a dampness clinging to the earth and making the air smell rich and tangy. As I gazed across the island I felt a sliver of sunlight fall across my face. I closed my eyes, taking a moment to welcome its gentle warmth. I remember thinking to myself that this might be the last chance I got to appreciate the sunshine.

You are probably wondering what it feels like, to know you are going to die. Was I afraid? Perhaps a little. But I mostly felt determined. I focused all my energy on the only thing that mattered – my child. He would live. He must.

My sisters stayed with me all night, until dawn had spread her rosy fingers across the sky. I cannot even remember what we spent our last hours chatting about. I just remember that they were mindlessly wonderful conversations, which had us in fits of laughter, despite my looming fate hanging over us. In the morning they were reluctant to leave, of course they were. I nearly broke down in tears myself trying to force them to go. But eventually, they relented, after promising again that they would be there for my child when the time came. Always.

As I watched them fly off for that final time, I did not feel sad, but rather thankful. Thankful that I had been able to reconcile with my sisters before the end, that I had had the chance to hold them one last time and tell them how much they meant to me. It is those little moments of closure that make facing your death so much easier.

I coaxed the dying fire back to life, knowing that the smoke would draw my killer to me quicker. No point delaying the inevitable. As I prodded the idle flames, I whispered the same words, like a prayer, "You'll be okay, I promise."

After a time, a weariness overcame me, so I shuffled my way back into the depth of the cave, finding comfort in the cool darkness, accompanied only by the motionless bodies of my previous victims. In the silence that followed, I heard the familiar voices crawling into my ear.

Powerful Medusa.

We will defeat him.

We will kill him.

He does not stand a chance against you.

I sighed, pressing my head back against the cold, damp wall. It seemed I would never escape these voices, not completely anyway. Perhaps if I had not been destined to die at the hands of this hero, then I might have eventually been driven insane by the snakes. I am glad I never got the chance to find out.

My snakes pricked up at a faint fluttering sound outside, one I had heard twice before in my life: Hermes' winged sandals. I knew immediately what this meant – my killer was here.

Without hesitation, I went to meet him.

"You must be Perseus."

He had his back to me and in one hand he held a sword, its curved edge winking threateningly in the glow of the dying fire. In his other hand, he held a shield that glittered with an unearthly shine. The gift of Athena.

He said nothing, but simply cocked his head slightly. What was wrong with him? Was he stupid? Or deaf? I took a slight step forward but still he did not turn to meet me. What was he playing at? Suddenly, my eyes found his. He had been staring directly at me through the reflection of his mirrored shield. My eyes burned with defensive ferocity, but I realised that in the reflection my deadly stare was useless.

Mirrors. My Achilles' heel, so to speak. I should have known Athena would embed some kind of flaw within my powers, a weakness she could expose and destroy me with using one of her beloved heroes. Now it made total sense why she had gifted Perseus this shield.

The silence stretched taught around us as our eyes remained locked.

Attack.

Kill.

Do it, Medusa!

"So, Perseus, you have come to kill me," I finally said, my gaze unwavering. He flinched slightly at the sound of his name, but continued to hold his ground. What was he waiting for?

"Nobody told me…" His voice was softer than I had expected. "That you would be…" His hazel eyes focused on my swollen stomach.

"What's the matter? Never seen a pregnant monster before?" I laughed emptily. Perseus shifted awkwardly, seeming unsure what to do. His reluctance fascinated me, never had a man hesitated like this before – they either simply attacked or fled. But they never *paused for thought*.

"You are not what I expected," he said finally, his eyes finding mine in the gleam of the shield, the firelight etched against his handsome features. His face was strong, yet somehow delicate at the same time.

"How so?"

"I did not expect a monster to be so...human," he admitted and despite myself I couldn't help but let out another sharp laugh. "How did this happen to you?" The question caught me off guard, nobody had ever bothered to ask me this before. For a moment I was lost for words.

"A lot of bad luck," I managed after a short pause. He nodded slowly, another tense silence settling uneasily between us. We were both poised and ready to attack, yet neither seemed to want to make the first move. Or was he simply lulling me into a false sense of security?

"Who is the father? If you don't mind me asking..." Perseus eventually enquired, another unexpected question. What was he stalling for? Or was he checking there was not another monster lurking further inside the cave?

"A man whom I hope to never meet again," I responded and he nodded slowly, seeming to understand the sentiment behind my words.

"I'm sorry to hear that."

"So, what is your plan for killing me?" I shrugged off his response, finding his sincerity disconcerting. "You do have a plan, don't you?" He glanced at his sword, as if he had completely forgotten it was there. He reaffirmed his grip on the handle, the muscles in his arm twitching.

"Well…" He stared back into the reflective shield. "Admittedly, I am not so sure anymore."

"That doesn't sound very heroic of you." My words were flecked with sarcasm.

"No, it doesn't, does it?" To my surprise he let out a slight chuckle. "To be honest, Medusa, I was expecting a crazed, ravenous monster… I mean, a monster I can kill easy, no problem…but an unarmed, pregnant…woman." I was silenced by his words, feeling strangely overwhelmed by the term 'woman'. Is that really how he saw me? A glimmer of hope struck somewhere deep inside me. "The problem is… I really need your head."

"Ah, that is a problem."

"Quite." He paused to think for a moment. "Perhaps you have an evil, identical twin I could slay instead?"

"Sadly not."

We stood in another silence, both incredulous at the situation unfolding around us – it seemed neither of us were what the other had expected. Perhaps, I thought to myself, my plan stood a chance after all. Either way, I had to try.

"What if we were to strike a deal?" I finally asked.

"It's a deal that got me in this situation in the first place."

"Just listen. You want my head, but you don't want to kill a pregnant woman." I chose my words carefully. "And all I want is for my child to live. So what if we make an agreement, that you let me live long enough for my child to be born and then you can have my head."

"You mean you would voluntarily let me behead you?" Perseus asked disbelievingly. "Now, that really doesn't sound very heroic of me, does it?"

"More heroic than beheading an unarmed pregnant woman," I replied evenly. It felt nice, reclaiming that title for myself

– woman. This made Perseus pause for thought and I felt my whole body tense up in the uncertain silence that followed. *Please let my child live. Please.*

"When are you due?" he eventually asked.

"Any day now, I'd say."

"Okay." He nodded slowly. "But on one condition. When the time comes we must face each other off as equals. I don't want you going easy on me, alright?"

"Of course." I tried to curb the relief from my voice; I did not want him to know how much power he held having the Fates on his side. It was safer if he thought us as equals.

"But you have to stay here, in this cave. I can't have you sneaking off or anything."

"I think my sneaking days are well behind me." I motioned to my ballooned stomach.

"Yes, well..." For a moment, Perseus looked at a loss. His courageous plan had just unravelled around him and now he was left uncertain and exposed. "I'm just, uh, going to stand guard at the mouth of the cave...you know, to make sure you don't escape and, uh, that nobody else comes for you."

"Okay then."

"Okay then."

And that was the start of our friendship.

Friends.

"Do you want anything?" Perseus asked later that same day, standing at the mouth of the cave with his back to me.

"What?"

"Do you want anything…food, water, anything like that?" I stared incredulously at the back of his head, his light curls glinting in the cold sunlight.

"Why?" This act of apparent kindness unnerved me.

"What do you mean 'why'?" He could not help but chuckle.

"I don't need anything. I'm fine," I replied with instinctive defensiveness.

"Suit yourself. I'm going to explore the island, see what there is to hunt around here." He picked up his sword and began to head off.

"Firewood," I suddenly called after him, "I need firewood."

"Firewood," he repeated as he walked away.

What strange dynamic was this? My killer doing *favours* for me? I let out a small laugh to myself, shaking my head incredulously.

"Perhaps this could actually work," I murmured to myself, feeling that flicker of hope burning inside me, fragile yet enduring.

Those first few days were wrapped in a tense silence. We made a point of staying out of each other's way, yet kept a constant eye on one another. Perseus always had his weapons close by and the man just did not seem to ever sleep. He was always wide awake, constantly alert. At first, I was reluctant to do so myself, but after a time the exhaustion of pregnancy got the better of me and I gave up battling the release of sleep. I had to blindly trust that this stranger was a man of his word, which I knew was a dangerous gamble. I would always wake with a jolt, my hands at my throat, expecting to find Perseus looming over me, ready to strike. But it never happened. Instead, I would awaken to the innocent sound of Perseus' absentminded whistling, as he busied himself with various tasks.

I discovered quickly that Perseus was terrible at sitting still. He had an endless buzz of energy about him, it was tiring just to watch him flitting between his various distractions. I wanted to find him annoying, but his energetic company was a welcome respite from the loneliness I had endured for so long. I would steal occasional glances when he was engrossed in a task, finding myself smiling as I watched his face knit together in concentration. I can still picture the way his tongue peeked out the corner of his mouth when he was really focused on something. The thought makes me smile even now.

As the days passed, I felt the tension inside me unravelling and I began to soften. I found my mood had lightened considerably, I was smiling more and sleeping better than I had in months. What was this effect Perseus' company was having on me? Before you even ask, I will tell you that I was *not* falling in love with Perseus. Of course he was attractive, all the heroes were. But there was more to Perseus than his looks. There was a genuineness about him that seemed to warm whatever space he filled. I had never met anyone like him.

"So, what was it then?" he finally asked, after a third silent day had passed by. The sky was swollen with sinister clouds, the atmosphere felt heavy and hot with the promise of rain. Perseus was busy whittling, his strong hands working the wood methodically. As usual, he had propped up the mirrored shield near the entrance of the cave so that he could keep an eye on me.

"What?" I had grown used to the silence that had settled between us, conversation felt like new and dangerous territory.

"You said you had had some bad luck." He flickered his eyes to mine within the reflective shield. "I would like to hear about it, if you wouldn't mind." There was a sincerity about him that always caught me off guard. I had spent so much of my life ignored and unwanted, I was not used to this kind of warm openness.

"It's a long story," I dismissed, making small circles across my stomach with my fingertips. I winced as I felt my son shifting inside me; perhaps he could sense my sudden uneasiness.

"It seems we have got the time." A grin was tucked away at the corner of Perseus' lips.

"It's depressing too."

"I'm a big boy, I think I can handle it."

"It is also none of your business." I felt guilty for the unnecessary edge to my voice, but defensiveness was second nature to me, as natural as taking a breath between sentences. Perseus shrugged, seemingly indifferent to my tone as he continued with his task. After a moment he paused, letting out a sigh with a shake of his head. He then balled his free hand into a fist and pressed it thoughtfully against his lips. He looked as if he were having a heated internal debate with himself.

"Was it bad enough to justify killing all those men?" he finally asked and I immediately sensed this question had been weighing on him for a while. I remained silent, watching him fidget restlessly in the reflection of the shield. "I've seen them in there, you know. All those statues…all those *bodies*."

"I wasn't trying to hide them," I countered.

"Did they honestly all deserve to die?"

Of course, you fool. There was a faint, irritable hiss in my ear.

"They came looking for me," I replied levelly. "It was kill or be killed. I had to protect myself…my son. What would you have done?"

"And what about before that?" Perseus' eyes narrowed as his fingernails scratched at the wood in his hands, dragging up jagged splinters. "I have heard of all your victims… I have even heard you kill children too…"

"Once." I flinched at his words. The memory I had suffocated for so long cut sharply into my mind, gasping for air. "And that was an accident."

"And what about all the others? Accidents too?"

"*They* were the real monsters," I snapped, feeling the irritation glow hot across my skin. "But you wouldn't understand. How could you? People like you get everything they ever wanted handed to them by the Gods. Your fate is laid out so perfectly you do not even have to look where you step." Perseus mouth twitched slightly, but he remained silent. "You kill and you are deemed a hero, celebrated by all, rewarded by the Gods… Yet when I kill I am immediately branded a monster, disgusting, wretched." I paused, drawing in an uneven breath as I let my words burn between us. "You will never know what it feels like to have the whole world against you, to be forced into a narrative you never wanted to be part of… So do not sit there and make assumptions about me, because you know nothing of what I have been through."

"Tell me then." Perseus' voice had softened considerably, but his gaze remained firm, unwavering.

"Why should I?" I tried to ease the frustration from my voice, irritated that I had let him rile me up so quickly.

"So that maybe I can understand."

"I do not have to explain anything to you." I turned away.

"You are right, you don't," Perseus sighed, placing his whittling tools to one side and rising to his feet. "I am going to go for a walk… I think perhaps you would prefer to be left alone for a while."

As I watched him leave I felt anger simmering inside me. It awakened the hateful thoughts that lurked within the darkest corners of my mind, smothering the previous warmth I had felt towards Perseus. I remember thinking to myself: what right did he have to judge me? A man who had been blessed by the Fates to live a heroic and celebrated life. A man loved by the Gods and showered with gifts and guidance whenever he needed it. The world had welcomed him with open arms; so of course he could be 'the good guy', he had never been forced to be anything else. What did he know of suffering? What did he know of pain? He judged me for the blood on my hands and yet was not his sole purpose in coming here to murder me? Or did he think his bloodshed worthy because the Gods deemed it so? Which was deeply ironic considering the Gods were the cruellest killers of them all. Perhaps if Perseus knew the truth about his precious Gods, then he would think differently about which side he was fighting for. Did he have any idea what Athena was really capable of, or had she blinded him with her sickening favouritism?

I paced inside the cave as these thoughts raged inside me. Outside, the swollen sky suddenly split open with a thunderous clap of lightning, as sheets of rain began to spill out, finally relieving the heaviness in the air.

You should kill him, Medusa.

Kill Perseus.

My anger had even roused the snakes. They slithered and writhed excitedly, their hissing faint yet persistent.

Kill him, Medusa.

He deserves to die.

They all do.

"Stop it." I batted away their heads as they swarmed around me. "I am not listening to you anymore."

You know you want to, Medusa.

You know we are right.

We are always right.

I stopped pacing and felt my fury fizzing through my veins, as a thought darkened my mind: *Could* I kill him? Surely not, as the Fates had already decided for us...but, could I at least try? Had I not killed countless men before just like him?

Yes, Medusa! Do it!

You could defy the Fates.

We believe in you.

Suddenly, I felt my child shift inside me, forcing my thoughts to sharpen back into harsh reality. What was I thinking? Of course I could not kill Perseus, to do so would only be sealing my fate sooner and putting my child's life at risk. I had to honour our agreement for as long as he would, that was the only way to protect my son. How could I be selfish enough to let my anger put him at risk? I silently cursed myself for letting the snakes infect my mind so easily. It seemed their toxic hold would never relent.

Another flash of lightning illuminated the cave, throwing grotesque shadows across the walls. I caught sight of Perseus sitting outside; he was back to whittling his wood, despite the rain falling heavily around him. I watched him silently for a few moments, as he tried to work the sodden wood and began to whistle contentedly to himself.

Gradually, I felt the downpour dampen my rage, causing it to gently ebb away, replaced instead by an overwhelming sense of exhaustion. I was tired of feeling angry, tired of hating and being hated, tired of this bitterness that had consumed me. What I would have given to rid myself of those poisons, to be as carefree as Perseus whistling cheerfully to himself in the midst of a thunderstorm. I realised in that moment that I should not hate Perseus for being happy, just because I could not be. None of this was his fault, any more than it was my own.

"Do you want to come inside?" My voice was lost in the hissing downpour, but Perseus must have heard something because he turned and approached me, with his eyes lowered. "Do you want to come in?" I repeated once he was closer. He hesitated for a moment, he had never stepped foot inside the cave since our initial meeting, to do so felt like an uneasy crossing of the invisible lines we had drawn between one another.

"Are you sure?" he asked, his eyes still set on the ground.

"If you want to." Without waiting for him to respond I went back inside and began to gather wood for a fire. As I coaxed the flames to life, I glanced over to Perseus, but he seemed to have disappeared. I assumed he had decided to reject my offer and felt a strange sense of disappointment flicker inside me. Why had I been disappointed? Just a moment ago I had been considering murdering this man. I shook my head at my own ridiculousness, laughing quietly to myself.

After a few moments, Perseus appeared inside the cave, carrying his sword and shield. He caught me eyeing the weapons and shifted uneasily.

"Just precautionary," he said, almost apologetically. He placed the sword down and set the shield up against the cave wall, so he could sit away but still keep an eye on me within its reflection.

Perseus had been soaked right through from the downpour; his clothes were moulded to his body, his hair sticking against his face. I might have imagined it, but I could have sworn he was shivering. As the fire came to life it filled the cave with a comforting glow and I saw Perseus began to relax a little within its warmth. For a while we sat in silence and I watched as Perseus' shadow flickered across the cave wall, like some distorted creature dancing to the sound of the crackling flames. I could feel his eyes watching me from within the shield, but I tried to ignore his scrutiny and instead focused my mind on the soothing sound of the rainfall outside.

"I just wanted to say, for the record," Perseus finally spoke, his voice was gentle yet sounded loud against the lengthy silence, "that I have not had everything just handed to me... I've faced some hardships too, you know." I instinctively made a dismissive noise at the back of my throat, like a choked laugh.

"So the Gods didn't just gift you that divine shield and sword? Or those winged sandals?" I threw him a challenging look within the shield, which was now glowing red with the reflection of the fire.

"That was different." Perseus shifted uneasily. "That was the first time I had ever experienced anything like that... I had never met a God in my life and suddenly there was Hermes...and then Athena, right there in front of me." He looked dazed just from the memory of the encounter. "They started telling me all about my fate...and then before I knew it they were handing me these gifts and giving me all this advice..." He shook his head incredulously.

"You are right." I nodded, my voice curled with sarcasm. "It sounds like you have endured some real hardships."

"You got angry when I made assumptions about you and yet here you are doing the exact same to me." He stared at my reflection pointedly as the flickering shadows carved out his features, distorting his beauty.

161

"Well, prove it to me then," I challenged, folding my arms expectantly.

"Alright."

And so, without further encouragement, he began to talk. He spoke with such openness and vulnerability I could not believe it at first. I thought he must have been lying, perhaps in an attempt to get my guard down and lull me into a false sense of security. Why else would he be so voluntarily honest with his enemy? And yet, there was such sincerity in his voice and as he spoke I felt something loosening in the air, easing the tension that had been constricting the space between us.

He told me about being rejected by his grandfather at birth and being thrown into the sea to die. Unwanted and abandoned by his own family. Of course, I knew all too well what that felt like. He talked about how his mother had saved them and raised Perseus by herself on an unfamiliar land. As he spoke I could feel his love and adoration for Danaë like a tangible warmth glowing inside me, making even the fire seem cold in comparison. I clasped my hands over my stomach and wondered what it would feel like to be so loved by your own child. If only one day I could have found out for myself.

Perseus continued to speak about his childhood and his humble yet happy life on Seriphos. He said he owed everything to his mother and his voice caught when he told me of the abuse Danaë had endured. At points he began to weep quietly and unashamedly. I had never seen a man cry like that before and it was beautiful to see such unapologetic vulnerability. Perseus even admitted to me that Danaë would often wake in the night screaming and described how he would always be there ready to comfort her.

"Is that why you never sleep?" I asked.

"Perhaps." He nodded with a sad smile.

He explained that he had vowed to protect his mother no matter the cost and of his deal with Polydectes. As I listened, I considered this agreement Perseus had fallen into and asked gently if he understood why Polydectes had really sent him here.

"He wants me dead, of course." Perseus nodded solemnly. "Though he won't get rid of me that easily."

When Perseus had finished talking the rain outside had eased and the fire had died down to delicate glowing embers. We sat in a comfortable silence for a little while, as I considered Perseus' words. Then, I did something I had never done before. I told him my own story. I am surprised even now at how exposed I allowed myself to be with a practical stranger, a man who was supposedly my rival, destined to end my life. But Perseus' words had opened up a space of trust between us, laying down a foundation for us both to feel safe to speak freely. As I talked, Perseus listened intently, the stillest he had been since I met him. He did not interject or ask questions, he just let my words flow out, like blood gushing from a wound. It felt cathartic, to form my pain into words and release each one from my body. I realised I had been holding so much in for so long, pushing it deep down and suffocating myself from the inside.

When I finally finished, I noticed Perseus was crying again.

"Are you okay?" I asked, after a pause. His light curls, now dry, quivered as he shook his head.

"I'm just… I am sorry."

"Me too."

I think we both found some sort of comfort within one another's suffering. We had been from seemingly such different worlds and yet in reality our lives were not so far apart at all. I think Perseus' experience with his own mother's abuse allowed him to understand me in a way so few people ever had.

163

"You are a survivor," he told me, "like my mother."

We did not stop talking.

We talked through the night, about everything and anything, our lives, our fears, our hopes and dreams, even our darkest thoughts. I don't think I had ever spoken so much in my life, but it felt so unbelievably freeing, to be able to speak so openly and unreservedly to another person. To be not only heard, but understood. I even told Perseus about the little boy, something I had never spoken to anyone about, not even my sisters.

"It was an accident," he said gently and I felt relief overwhelm me, moving me to tears. How deeply I had needed to hear that, to have someone affirm it for me.

Somehow, in the midst of all those feelings spoken and stories shared, a friendship unfurled between us. It might seem strange to you, that I befriended the man destined to kill me – believe me, it was strange for me too. I can assure you that I did not *want* to like Perseus; it would have made things so much easier if I had just carried on hating him.

"Well," Perseus sighed, as we watched Helios setting off on yet another journey.

"Well, what?" My voice had been hoarse from talking all night.

"This certainly complicates things, doesn't it?"

"I guess it does."

Fate.

Our friendship blossomed as the days passed and I found it hard to believe I had only known Perseus a week; it quickly felt as if I had known him my whole life. You might find this extreme, but some friendships are just like that – you can find the bond of a lifetime in just a matter of days. I hope you will all be lucky enough to experience a friendship like that one day.

The weather was relentlessly miserable, so we spent most of our time in the cave, enjoying the simple pleasure of one another's company. During the occasional periods the rain subsided we would venture out for walks. I say 'walks', but really Perseus was the only one actually walking, whilst I waddled embarrassingly slowly beside him, like some oversized heifer. Of course, Perseus was endlessly patient with me, insisting he did not mind the 'leisurely' pace.

"You get to see more of the sights when you take things slow," he assured me with a smile.

I remember I felt genuinely happy, which may sound daft considering my fate was looming before me, cold and resolute. But, at times, the weight of our future seemed to simply melt away, replaced by a wonderful contentedness I had not felt since childhood. Of course, this feeling could only ever be short lived, but perhaps that is what made it all the more special.

After a while, however, I could sense Perseus growing restless.

He became quieter and his mood uncharacteristically darker. He began to spend more time away from the cave, making vague excuses in order to keep his distance from me. I could not take offence to his behaviour, I knew he was struggling with our intertwined fate. He did not want to be a killer any more than I had wanted to be a monster.

After nearly a fortnight had passed, I found him outside the cave packing his belongings. I had immediately known something was wrong that day, as I had not been woken by his usual cheerful whistling.

"What's going on?" I asked, trying to keep my voice light.

"I'm going home," he said as he stuffed his items into his worn leather bag.

"You're leaving? But what about our deal?"

"Our deal?" He kept his gaze on the ground. "You mean our deal for me to kill you? Medusa, we both know I can't do that."

"But, you have to." I felt a twinge in my chest.

"No I don't. I'm not going to kill you." He sounded irritated, his hands fumbled as he packed and repacked the same few items.

"It is the will of the Fates, Perseus."

"I was told I was destined to behead a monster, not-" he gestured vaguely towards me.

"And what of your mother and Polydectes?"

"I will deal with him another way."

I sighed, deflated. Of course, I should have been encouraging Perseus to go, urging him off my island as quickly as I could. But in all honesty, I could not bear the thought of losing him. Other than my sisters, he was the only friend I had ever had.

"You deserve a life, Medusa," he said, rising to his feet and shifting the bag over his shoulder. He kept his eyes lowered. "You deserve to be happy. To know your child."

"I just…" My voice trembled. In that moment, I wished more than anything he could look at me. "I don't think those things are part of the plan for me, Perseus."

"Well, if you want to die, then fine." He was trying to suppress his anger now, but I could see the muscle in his jaw twitching. "But I am not going to kill you."

"Yes, you are."

The cold voice rang out around us and I saw the colour drain from Perseus' face. It was a voice we both immediately recognised and one we could never forget.

Athena.

She appeared beside us, her towering frame belittling even Perseus. Her armour blazed brilliantly in the sunlight, yet it appeared dull compared to her flashing grey eyes. Her presence sent a chill right through me, forcing me back to that temple floor, where I had lain at her feet all that time ago – broken, hopeless.

"What is the meaning of this, Perseus?" The air sparked around her as she rounded on him. "Why is *she* still alive? I empowered you with great weapons to slay this monster and yet here she stands, her head still attached."

"I apologise, my great Goddess, but there must be some mistake for I do not see a monster here," Perseus replied. His voice was calm but I could see the sweat prickling across his forehead.

"Foolish boy," she scorned, "you have no idea what she is capable of."

"We have a deal," I interjected, trying to draw Athena's wrath away from Perseus. Her cutting eyes darted to me as I spoke. "Once my child is born, he will kill me. I assure you, Athena."

"A deal?" she spat at me dismissively. "Heroes do not make deals with monsters."

"I am sorry my Goddess." Perseus bowed his head. "I cannot fulfil your request. You will have to find another hero to do your bidding." His words caused a rumble of anger to rip from Athena, trembling the ground beneath us. I winced, terrified of what Athena might do to Perseus for refusing her will.

"You will kill her or I will kill you," she warned, her voice sharp as a blade.

"Perseus, don't-"

"Quiet you," she snarled, not even bothering to look at me, "your temptress ways cannot work anymore."

"I will kill a monster for you, my Goddess, any monster you like." Perseus did his best to meet Athena's blistering glare. "But I will not kill a pregnant woman."

"She is not a woman!" Athena let out a bark of ugly laughter, but Perseus remained impassive. After a pause, Athena inhaled sharply, her expression shifting as she decided to change her tactic. "You are destined for great things, Perseus." Athena's words suddenly flowed like velvet, rich and seductive. "You will be one of the greatest heroes who ever lived. You will live a long and successful life, with a beautiful, adoring wife. You will bear children who will become famous kings and heroes. History will remember you, you will be celebrated throughout generations." I saw something catch in Perseus' eyes as she spoke. "But only if you act *now*. If you refuse and choose to return home empty handed, then that destiny will be lost forever. You will be cursed to live a miserable life, dying alone and forgotten…" Athena drew back, allowing her words to settle heavily on Perseus' shoulders. "So, what will it be?"

I could see a vein pulsing in Perseus' neck, his face gathered together in deep thought. The seconds dragged out endlessly. I wanted to say something, to warn Perseus of the dangers of refusing Athena. But I knew my interruption would only make matters worse.

Finally, Perseus spoke, his words slow and resolute, "I will not kill her."

"Do it or I will make your mother die a slow and painful death," Athena spat, her previous composure slipping. I saw fury flash in Perseus' eyes at the mention of his mother; he opened his mouth to retaliate but his words were drowned out by the howl of pain that suddenly ripped from my body.

"Medusa, what is it?" he asked without looking at me. "Are you okay?"

"The baby," I gasped, feeling a warm liquid running down my legs, "I think the baby is coming."

"Oh, wonderful," Athena hissed sardonically, rolling her eyes.

"Please, Athena." My voice was ragged, as I tried to manage the pain convulsing through my body. "Please, let me have my child. And then Perseus can kill me. Please. That's all I ask."

Athena regarded me with her steely grey eyes, her expression was unreadable. "I should kill you right now before your little runts ever see the light of day," she hissed, before turning back to Perseus. "If she is not dead by sundown, then I will make sure your own mother is." She vanished in a flash of brilliant light, her cold threat lingering in the space where she had just stood.

"Medusa!" Perseus rushed towards me keeping his eyes averted, but I immediately placed my hand out, halting him in his place.

"No, wait," I spoke through gritted teeth, as the pain gripped my entire body. "I have to do this alone."

"But-"

"Please. Let me do this alone." Without waiting for him to respond, I turned and staggered back into the cave.

Great Medusa.
Powerful Medusa.
You can do this.
We believe in you.

Twins.

Childbirth is a wondrous thing. Of course, it was hideously painful, there is no denying that, but I found the pain strangely exhilarating. It made me feel powerful, godlike even, to create life from inside me. To this day I am still amazed that women all around the world are able to tear themselves apart to form life. And yet men still think that they are the stronger sex... I mean, honestly.

Afterward, I lay in exhausted bliss, blanketed in the clammy warmth of the cave. I cradled my babies like little trophies, one in each arm. Twin boys. Yes, it was a surprise to me too. All that time I had been talking to one baby, when really two had been listening.

My boys.

My children.

They might not have been what you would traditionally expect from twins, one being winged and hoofed and all, but I suppose that is what happens when you are related to the Gods. Regardless, they were both utterly perfect to me. I could not stop looking at them. My sons.

"We finally meet." I smiled down at their scrunched little faces, blinking away overwhelmed tears. It was all too much... it still is...

You will have to forgive me, but I cannot really put into words how I felt in that moment. Just thinking about it is difficult for me, even now. Like a broken part of me that has healed crooked, it will always be painful. But though it hurts, I would not trade that memory for anything in the world. I have relived it so many times over in my head. That little pocket of time, a tiny moment of perfection I have all to myself. Nobody can take that away from me. I keep it safe inside, tucked away so that the darkness of my past cannot corrupt it. It is the only comfort I have. Bittersweet.

"I am sorry we don't have more time," I whispered to them softly, shifting a little to bring their faces closer to mine. As I gazed down at them, I imagined their lives unfolding before me and felt the painful realisation ache through my chest – I would never share any of it with them. They would live their lives never knowing their mother.

But, they would *live*. That was what mattered, that was all that ever mattered. They would live, even if I would not.

"You probably won't even remember me, will you?" I cooed and they gurgled in response, their sleepy eyes blinking slowly. "But if you remember one thing from this moment, remember that you are loved and you will always be loved. Can you do that for me? Will you remember?" But they were already both fast asleep, their little faces so beautifully peaceful, so innocent. As I watched them quietly snooze, I felt silent tears stream down my cheeks.

Just a handful of minutes, that was all I got.

I told you time was never a friend of mine.

Death.

You might wonder, why was Athena so adamant Perseus fulfilled his destiny? Why did she even care? Well, like I said before, Athena liked to champion heroes. But only the greatest of heroes were good enough for her divine help and she prided herself in being able to identify the very best of the best. She could not have Perseus ruin her track record by messing that up. Let's not forget that Athena was hardly my biggest fan either, so it was a win-win for her.

You might also be feeling frustrated that I accepted my fate so readily, wondering, should I not have at least tried to fight back? But honestly, there was no point. I had no chance, no choice. Even if Perseus and I had tried to delay our fate, the conclusion would have always been the same, no matter what course we took. Perseus would kill me; the Fates had decided and thus it must be so.

Helios' chariot was starting to dip below the horizon when I finally emerged from the cave. Perseus had been waiting anxiously outside, the ground muddy and worn from his endless pacing. I saw his sigh of pure relief as he caught sight of me in his shield.

"Are you okay?" he asked softly and I nodded, meeting the reflection of his eyes. He looked so very tired. "And the baby?"

"Bab*ies*." I smiled. "Two boys." He opened his mouth to speak, but seemed at a loss for words. He could only manage a trembling smile. "Afterward, I need you to do something for me. I need you to take them to my sisters."

"Medusa I-"

"Please listen, we don't have much time." I tried to keep my voice steady. "They're on the island just to the north of this one. You can't miss it. I need you to promise me you will take my children to them. Please."

"I promise."

A heavy silence settled over us as we watched the sunlight bleeding out across the horizon. I could feel Perseus' guilt hanging between us like a tangible weight in the air. All that pain and remorse he just couldn't form into words.

In all honesty, I felt sorry for him. He did not want to be the hero of this story just as much as I did not want to be the villain. We were both victims of the Fates' cruel ruling. I wonder if they had been watching us, I can just imagine their smug faces as they cackled loudly to one another, marvelling at their cruel handiwork.

"It's okay," I finally whispered, my voice calm.

You might not believe me, but in that moment, I didn't feel afraid. In fact, I felt an overwhelming sense of triumph. My children were alive and safe; I had saved them. I finally had lived up to my name: *Protector*. Perhaps this was how it was always meant to be, my life in exchange for theirs. Well, that was a trade I would willingly accept.

No, Medusa!

Don't let us die!

Fight back!

I ignored the angry hissing flickering in my ear. It was too

174

late to be swayed by the snakes now – my mind was already made up. I was tired of running, tired of fighting. It was time to accept my fate.

I watched Perseus pick up his sword with his spare hand, nervously flexing his fingers around the handle. As always, he stood with his back to me, but I could see the reflection of his ashen face within his shield. It did not surprise me to see he was crying, his eyes filled with unbridled pain. I loved that Perseus wore his emotions so unashamedly, it was one of the most beautiful things about him.

"I don't think I can…"

A change in the air stopped him from finishing his sentence. That familiar prickling sensation crawled across my skin, the tense atmosphere was suddenly charged by something else entirely. Athena had returned.

She materialised beside Perseus, making him appear like a child in her looming shadow. Athena was muttering something to him heatedly, but he was just shaking his head, his face shadowed with a heavy reluctance.

"Athena." My directness seemed to surprise her. She snapped her head up, her grey eyes flashing. Those eyes I had once admired. "I want to talk to you."

"You dare address me?" I could feel the ground humming beneath my feet as she advanced on me.

"I want to talk to you," I repeated, my voice level. "I will make sure Perseus kills me."

"How?"

"Just believe me, I will make sure of it." She curled back her lips in a disdainful snarl, but said nothing. I could see in the distance Perseus was shaking his head. I ignored him and continued. "I will make sure of it, if you promise me this – leave my children alone. Do not let the Gods subject them to the pain and suffering you forced on me."

"You're trying to make a deal with me?" Athena seethed, her armour glinting in the dying sunlight. "Who do you think you are?"

"I am the monster standing in the way of your hero fulfilling his destiny," I countered calmly. "I know the outcome you want and I can make it happen."

"I have no interest in your pathetic children." She raised her chin defiantly. "Besides, you have no power against the Fates, Perseus will kill you regardless."

"Yes, he will," I agreed, my gaze unwavering, "but perhaps it won't be today, or tomorrow. It might not even be for many summers to come. The Fates are binding but they are also vague and destinies can always be blown off course. You know that as well as anyone."

"You are as insolent as ever." Her eyes narrowed, though something in her expression had shifted, as if she were suddenly regarding me in a new light. I knew this was very dangerous territory and still I pressed on.

"All I ask is that you leave my children alone. Will you do it?"

"I have already told you, I do not care about your little runts," she said, tightening her grip on her spear warningly. "You should know better than to make a Goddess repeat herself." I knew this was the closest to a 'yes' I was ever going to get.

"And what of Danaë?" I urged.

"She will remain unharmed if Perseus fulfils his duties." Athena's eyes glowed with a cold fury.

"Good," I whispered, but she ignored me, already turning her attention back to Perseus.

"My tolerance is being tested to its limit, Perseus. You do not want to push me any further."

"Perseus," I called out to him, meeting his eyes in the reflection of the shield, "it's okay." Athena watched me approach Perseus with sharp eyes, but she remained silent. I think she had finally realised I was the only one who could get through to him, or perhaps she had simply grown tired of wasting her breath on insolent mortals.

I stopped just behind Perseus, the perfect distance for him to strike. He held my gaze in the shield, his eyes red-rimmed, lips trembling.

Don't do it, Medusa.
Don't kill us.
We must fight!
We must live!

"You have to do this, Perseus," I whispered. "For my children and for your mother... It is the only way we can protect them."

"But why does...?" He was unable to finish, his agony hung in the unspoken question.

"I don't know. But I will take the sacrifice. For my children. And for you."

The silence stilled around us as the last fragments of daylight clung to the horizon. I could feel Athena shifting beside us, as she made an irritated noise at the back of her throat. Her patience was wearing dangerously thin.

"Just don't miss, okay? The last thing I need is you messing this up." I smiled and despite himself Perseus let out a small laugh, flecked with his tears.

No, Medusa! Don't!

"Get on with it," Athena barked, but neither of us even acknowledged her, we kept our reflected eyes locked on one another's.

"Medusa, I'm sorry."

177

"I know."

The last thing I remember was the sadness in Perseus' eyes as he swung his sword and the stinging bite as it met my neck.

And then, it was over.

Beyond.

I have seen many depictions of my death. Perseus is always portrayed as the triumphant hero, handsome and powerful. Whilst I am continually reduced to nothing more than a gawping head, mouth hung slack like some kind of gruesome sex-doll. I am not bitter about it; I am beyond all that now. But really, would not the truth have made for a far more interesting image? Perseus' tear-streaked face, striking out remorsefully. Me, facing my death with a calm resolution. Athena overseeing the execution with those calculating grey eyes. Now, *that* is the masterpiece I want to see showcased in your galleries and museums.

Okay, perhaps I am still a little bitter about it, if I am completely honest.

But how can I not be? History has watered my death down into a dull cliché – 'the hero slays the monster'. Worse still, I have been robbed of any agency whatsoever, they didn't even have me put up a good fight. The popular version claims I was slain whilst sleeping. Even more infuriating are the accounts that tell of stupid Medusa being fooled by the shiny shield, as if I have never seen a reflection before. *Really*, that's the best you can come up with?

You will also find that any mention of my deal with Perseus has been scrubbed clean from history, Athena made sure of that. The story now goes that my children spilled from my severed body after my death. My one and only triumph in life has been substituted for a lifeless corpse. There is probably some kind of poetic symbolism in that, but really it just pisses me off.

Though, I cannot be surprised, can I? Athena would hardly want the world knowing about the mortal who found a loophole within her own fate and if people knew of my friendship with Perseus it might have risked tarnishing his legacy. Besides, I believe history preferred to remember me as a dehumanised monster, it made for a more 'suitable' story. Our fragile patriarchy could hardly accept a female monster who can kill men *and* think for herself. That would be far too scary, wouldn't it?

Anyway, where was I? Oh yes, I was dead.

You are probably wondering what it feels like to die. It is something we mortals have all wondered, at one time or another. Well, I am sorry to disappoint, but it is quite anticlimactic. It is like falling asleep; you are not really aware it has happened until afterwards.

I briefly felt the sword cut into my neck and then a rush of air escaped my body, like a sigh. After that, I simply felt nothing at all. What had happened? I remember asking myself. Had Perseus stopped himself? Had he not gone through with it after all?

"Well done," a voice spoke. Athena.

I looked up and saw that Perseus was staring directly at me. It was the first time he had ever looked me in the eyes. He had such beautiful eyes.

"Don't look!" I wanted to warn him, but my voice came out warped and muffled, as if I were speaking beneath muddy waters. "What is going on?" Perseus did not respond, he just kept staring. He had this strange, distant look in his eyes, one that I had never seen before. He swayed unsteadily, before collapsing heavily to his knees, a sob ripping from his chest. I instinctively moved forwards, throwing my arms around him and yet… I felt nothing, my hands brushed right through him. I tried to embrace him again and still nothing. A third time I attempted, still to no avail.

"I'm sorry." Perseus gulped out the words between sobs. He looked up and at the sight of his tortured eyes I felt something give way inside me.

"It's okay, Perseus. I'm here. It's okay," I told him. But he could not hear me; I could not reach him.

"Forgive me, Medusa," he whispered. It was then that I realised he had not been looking at me, but rather, beyond me. I turned to see Athena standing a little way behind us, her lips twitching into something reminiscent of a smile. I cautiously approached her, trying to make out what she and Perseus were looking at.

It was a body.

It was *my* body.

Limp, lifeless, headless. Dead.

As the heavy realization settled over me, I felt Athena turn beside me. I looked up to find her staring directly at me, her ghost of a smile hardening. I calmly held her gaze, somehow knowing she could see me, though Perseus could not. We stayed like that for a moment, then Athena gave a slight nod of her head. What did that nod mean? I wish I could tell you, believe me I have spent centuries endlessly wondering. Was it some form of acknowledgement of my sacrifice? A mark of respect even? Or was it just smug recognition that she had finally won? I guess I will never know.

"You took your time," a familiar voice came from behind me.

"What are you doing here?" I spun round to find Hermes standing before me, amusement flickering across his face.

181

"I have come to escort you." He gave a flamboyant bow.

"Escort me where?"

"I think you know where," Hermes said, staring pointedly at the headless body crumpled at our feet. Of course, how could I have forgotten? Alongside his other duties, Hermes was also responsible for shepherding souls to the afterlife. I should have known I would be seeing him again.

"I see," I said softly, gazing down at my severed head. My blood appeared almost black within the gathering darkness. "Why do I not feel afraid?"

"Because it is your time." Hermes' smile appeared genuine, perhaps for the first time ever.

"That makes sense," I murmured, distractedly glancing back at Perseus. He was still crying, but Athena was standing over him now, whispering something into his ear. Her voice sounded uncharacteristically warm. I felt an aching inside me – how deeply I wanted to be able to comfort him, to tell him everything was okay.

"I just love a sensitive guy, don't you?" Hermes followed my gaze over to Perseus, giving a longing sigh.

"Do we have to go right now?" I asked quietly, my attention drifting up to the cave where I knew my babies slept, peacefully unaware of the fact they had just lost their mother.

If I could just have one last look at them…

"I'm afraid so." Hermes' impossibly blue eyes sparkled as he offered out his hand, palm upright. "It is time to go." I hesitated slightly, my gaze lingering on the cave. My sons. "Medusa?"

"I know," I whispered.

I took Hermes' hand and felt the world slip away.

Limbo.

The next thing I remember was a coldness. It rattled right through me, like an icy breeze caught between my bones. For a while that was all there was, just the dark and the cold. I do not know how long I was like that for, like I have said before, time has no meaning for the dead. But at some point, the darkness around me began to come alive, shifting into murky shapes that shuffled past me, trudging towards some unknown destination. Where had Hermes gone? I was trying to make sense of what was going on, but the world around me felt disjointed, blurring at the edges and making it impossible to focus. So, I did all I could do, I let myself be carried along with the swell of shadows, marching ceaselessly onwards.

The walking felt endless, or perhaps it felt like no time at all, it is hard to explain. There was no detail or colour to distinguish the world around us, just the endless darkness, populated only by the shadowy figures lumbering forward. The main thing I noticed was how quiet it was, that kind of eerie stillness that makes you want to cry out, just so you can hear something again. That's when I realised – the snakes were completely silent, completely still. I instinctively moved to touch my hair but could no longer feel anything. It seemed they had not made the journey to the world beyond life. I guess that was one small silver lining of dying – a bit of peace and quiet.

Eventually, we reached a bottleneck where the dark figures

were being funnelled one by one. I tried to see where we were heading for, but I could not make out anything within the perpetual gloom. As we waited, I glanced at the shadows closest to me. If I stared hard enough I could just make out a wisp of detail caught in the depths of their ghostly faces – a pair of frightened eyes, a mouth contorted in anguish, a broken body. But as soon as they moved their faces were gone, swallowed up by the darkness.

What must I have looked like? I squinted downwards, trying to glimpse some familiarity, but my body was shadowy and indistinct, just like everyone else around me. I touched my face but felt nothing beneath my fingertips. I lowered my hands to my chest and still felt nothing. It was as if my body were entirely absent. Running my hands upwards, I realised all I could feel was a strange warmth emitting from my neck, at exactly the spot where Perseus had struck. I shuddered.

"Payment," a voice wheezed out when I finally reached the front of the queue. I glanced up, knowing immediately who I was facing – Charon, the ferryman of Hades, whose eternal duty was to carry souls across the River Styx to the afterlife.

Charon waited for me to respond and I could almost hear the dust rattling inside his ancient lungs. He was taller than I had expected, his sallow skin stretched taught over his skeletal body – it looked painful to be that thin. Charon's clothes were just moth-bitten rags, hanging limp from his long limbs. The holes where his eyes should have been were endless dark tunnels. He looked like a body that had been left out to rot.

"Well?" I wasn't sure if I imagined the creaking noise his bones made as he leant forward.

"I…I don't have any money." My voice sounded oddly disjointed from my body. Charon leant backwards and it looked as if it caused him great effort to move.

"Move aside," he rasped.

"But—"

"Payment." He was already addressing the shadow behind me, who had marched forward, shuffling me out of place. I watched as this soul opened his mouth and choked out a coin. He then handed this coin over and was ushered onto the narrow boat bobbing silently behind Charon, floating on a bed of darkness.

"But where am I to go?" I edged forward again, hearing an eerie groan from the queue of souls behind me. I don't know why they were in such a rush; it's not like any of us were short for time down here.

Charon did not respond, instead he pointed a knotted, bony, finger over my head. I turned and saw a clump of shadows gathered in the far corner, floating listlessly, heads bowed. The unburied. Souls who would never find their way across the River Styx, because they had never had a proper burial. Forever trapped in this limbo, cursed to never rest in peace.

Suddenly, it all made sense to me. Of course I had been left unburied. I had always known Perseus needed my head as his prize and who would bury a headless body? The ceremony probably would not have worked even if Perseus had tried. Yet, I have to admit, I still felt a pang of betrayal at having been left in this limbo. Shouldn't Hermes have warned me of this? Though, I suppose I knew better than to expect anything of him.

As I found my place amongst the unburied souls, I felt a panic begin to constrict inside me. Was this it now? Was this my eternity? Did I not deserve a little peace, even in death? Perhaps this was my final punishment from Athena.

All of a sudden, a flash of light cut into me, like a searing headache carving down my temples right the way through my body. I snapped open my eyes and found myself staring at a large man with an ugly, indignant sneer smeared across his face.

"Here is your prize." I heard Perseus' voice from somewhere behind me. I wanted to turn and call out to him, but I was locked onto this stranger's eyes, unable to break from his furious glare. Suddenly, that familiar chill rushed through me and I could not help but smile. How I had missed this feeling, this *power*.

A look of sudden blind panic flashed in the man's eyes as they began to crust over. He recoiled backwards in an attempt to escape me, but as he twisted away his whole body froze and hardened, forever trapping him in that desperate, contorted shape. I sensed a commotion around me and heard Perseus say something, but I was plunged back into darkness before I could make sense of it all.

And just like that, I was back in the depths of the Underworld. I registered the depressingly familiar gloom as my mind slowly processed what had just occurred. As it slowly dawned on me I began to laugh, unapologetically loud and triumphant.

He had done it.

Perseus had fulfilled his end of the bargain. He had taken my head to Polydectes and let him look into the eyes of the monster Medusa. Of course, the foolish King had not even considered my fatal stare could endure after death. His tiny mind could not fathom the idea of a dead woman yielding any kind of power.

And so, Perseus had defeated him.

No, *we* had defeated him. Together.

The End.

I appreciate I have been talking for a while now and I thank you for sparing your time, I know how precious it is for the living. But I started this story from the very beginning and it only seems fitting to finish at the very end.

Perseus was true to his word. He took my new-born sons and delivered them to Euryale and Stheno. He tried to explain the situation, but suffice to say, they were less than welcoming to the man who had just murdered their little sister. They attacked my killer in an attempt to avenge me, but fortunately for Perseus he had in his possession a helmet of invisibility, allowing him to vanish completely from my sisters' merciless grasp. This helmet was, of course, just another of his many divine gifts from the Gods.

Once he escaped my sisters, Perseus was able to finally continue his journey home to his beloved mother. But it was not a straight route back, it never is for heroes. Perseus encountered multiple challenges along his way, namely the Titan Atlas and the sea monster Cetus. But it was not all battles and bloodshed. Perseus also found love on his journey, when he saved the Ethiopian princess Andromeda. History remembers her as being extremely beautiful, but I like to think there was more to her than simply that.

Eventually, Perseus made it home to his anxiously awaiting mother. I imagine it was an emotional reunion, filled with hugs and tears and outpourings of love. I wish I could have been there to see it.

It did not take long for Perseus to discover King Polydectes had been harassing Danaë since the moment he left Seriphos. Without hesitation, Perseus took my head to the king and together we put an end to his pathetic life.

Once Polydectes had hardened to a lump of useless stone, Perseus felt he had satisfied the Fates and now all he wanted was to live his life in peace.

"Here you are, as promised." Down in the dark beyond, I somehow heard his voice, resonating inside me.

"Perseus!" I had called back desperately, feeling a rush of love and relief surge through me. How badly I had needed to hear a familiar voice. But my words fell flat, swallowed up by that perpetual, oppressive darkness. Wherever he was, he could not hear me. I have spent so much of my life not being heard.

"It will make a fearsome shield. One you should wear with pride." His voice in my head again. I realised he was talking to someone else. "And please, allow her to find peace. As we discussed."

"You two and your endless deals." Athena's voice flickered like a spark inside me. For the first time ever, she sounded in a good mood. Was she even *smiling*?

"I did everything you asked of me." That was Perseus again, his voice calm and collected. "This is all I ask in return. Please."

"It is already done," Athena responded, her voice growing distant.

"Well, fancy seeing you down here!" Another voice now, but this one was coming from right behind me. It was a voice I knew all too well and yet for the first time in my life I actually felt relieved to hear it.

"I'm beginning to think you are stalking me." I turned to see Hermes' broad grin. He looked even more out of place amongst the dead, his body emitting a warm glow that caused the shadowy souls to recoil. I could not help but return his smile; he was like a breath of fresh air down here. Do not get me wrong, I still disliked Hermes of course, but I hated that depressing limbo even more. It was a horrible, soul-sucking place. I think I would have even welcomed Athena's company as a respite from that miserable monotony.

"So how are you settling in? Making friends? I hope you are behaving yourself." Hermes cast his gaze across the shrinking shadows, a smirk catching somewhere between his lips and eyes.

"What are you doing here?" I sighed, narrowing my eyes. "Have you come to gloat? To laugh at the unburied? You could have warned me you know..."

"Gloat?" A mischievousness sparked in Hermes' eyes. "As much as gloating is one of my *favourite* pastimes, it is not the purpose of this visit." He looked around us and shuddered. "Gods, this place really is depressing, isn't it? I mean I know you are all dead, but would it kill you guys to smile?" The souls retreated further, spooked by Hermes' directness. "Well, anyway, I am actually here because I have a message."

"For me?" I felt a small swell of hope balloon in my chest.

"No, not you. For him." Hermes jerked his thumb over to Charon and I felt the hope inside me immediately dwindle. "He's not a fan of mine though, so I'm just stalling a little bit, warming myself up, you know?"

"Is anyone a fan of you?"

"Well, I thought we were at least friends!" Hermes gasped, placing his hand over his heart, as if my words had been a physical blow.

"Friends don't help other friends get their heads chopped off," I pointed out dryly.

"Really?" Hermes worked a look of mock surprise. "Well, clearly I need to rethink a few things…"

"What business do you have with Charon anyway?" At my words something flickered in Hermes' eyes, his lips curling into his usual conceited smile. If I had been alive, that look would have worried me, but now I was dead I honestly did not care. Nothing scares you when you are dead, which I suppose is one small positive.

"Why don't you come and find out?"

Hermes caused a great disturbance as he strode through the swell of fresh souls awaiting safe passage. The shadowy figures withdrew away from his glowing presence, ruining the formation of Charon's orderly queue. I followed in his disruptive wake, trying hard not to make eye contact with the disgruntled dead.

"Charon, old pal, it is good to see you again." Hermes beamed as he shoved the last soul aside. Charon tilted his head very slowly, the dark tunnels where his eyes should have been fixed on Hermes. I could have imagined it, but I swear I saw Charon stiffen slightly at the sight of him.

"Hermes." He drew in a rasping breath and it sounded like his entire insides had rusted over.

"You are looking well! Lost some weight? All that rowing I bet!" Hermes playfully jabbed an elbow towards Charon's emaciated body. He said nothing, but simply stared impassively at Hermes. To my surprise, Hermes seemed quite unsettled by Charon's silence; this was the first time I had seen his mask of confidence slip. He rushed to continue speaking, "Sadly I cannot stay to chitchat, old pal. I am actually here on business, you see. A request from Athena." He waited again for Charon to respond, but the ancient oarsman just continued to stare, his face eerily blank. "Right, well, Athena requests passage to the Underworld...for Medusa." Hermes suddenly shoved me forward, causing me to stagger slightly.

"For me?" I spluttered.

"Yes, for you." Hermes flashed me a look which could only be read as: *keep quiet.* "She needs the VIP treatment, straight to Asphodel Meadows. None of that judgement stuff."

"She cannot pay, she cannot pass," Charon responded, his breath rattling as he spoke.

"Here." Suddenly, a glittering gold coin appeared in Hermes' hand. "From Athena herself." He passed it to me, nodding his head towards Charon. Carefully, I placed the coin in Charon's thin, outstretched hand, not daring to hope that this might actually work.

If I'd still had breath in my body, I would have been holding it, as Hermes and I silently watched Charon inspect the coin, his thin mouth downturned. *Could* this actually work? I had spent so much of my life being disappointed, why should it be any different in death?

"There." He pocketed the coin and pointed a gnarled finger to an empty seat at the back of his boat. I could tell from his expression he was not too pleased about this arrangement.

"Th-thank you," was all I could manage, numbed by the overwhelming shock.

"Told you it would work." Hermes grinned, giving me a nudge.

"But why would Athena do this for me?"

Hermes let out a loud snort, which made a change from his usual, musical laugh. "She didn't do it for *you*, Athena would let you rot for all she cared. She did it for Perseus... I think he felt guilty for cutting off your head and all. Bless him." Charon banged his oar loudly and tilted towards the boat. "Better get in, you don't want to get on Bony's bad-side."

"But what of my sons? Will they be okay? Will they be happy?" The questions escaped me in a rush of desperation, but Charon was already ushering me forwards, blocking Hermes from view. I cursed myself for not asking these questions sooner, if only I had more time… Why was I always running out of it, even in death? Chronos, what is it you have against me?

As I clambered on board, I felt the weight of endless dead eyes all around me. It felt strange to have people be able to look at me again, it made me feel unnervingly exposed. Unsettled by this attention, I glanced back and was slightly comforted to see Hermes waving, his energetic enthusiasm contrasting comically with the desolate souls surrounding him.

"They grow up so fast!" He gave a flourish and started fake sobbing on the shoulder of a particularly confused soul, blowing his nose so loudly I think the whole of the Underworld must have heard. If Charon had eyes, I swear he would have been rolling them. Hermes must have sensed his hostile audience, so he called out, "Try not to miss me too much!" Then he quickly disappeared with a small pop of light.

"Don't worry, I won't," I muttered under my breath, but despite myself I was smiling.

With an unceremonious huff, Charon began to edge the boat away from the dock. I do not know how Charon's ancient body mustered up the power, but he rowed methodically, without missing a single beat. With each thrust we glided further into the heavy darkness, heading towards our final resting place, to that strange unknown.

You might have expected my life to flash before my eyes; it would seem a fitting time for it to do so. But I was not thinking about myself at all. Instead, as I made my final journey into the eternal world beyond, my mind was on one thing and one thing only: my sons.

Please Gods, let them live a good life. Let them be happy.

That was all that mattered.

Afterward.

I presume you would like to know what happened to everyone after my death?

Well, I am happy to confirm that Athena was telling the truth about Perseus' fate. He was blessed with the rare gift of a long and happy life, something so few heroes ever actually attain. As Athena had foretold, Perseus and Andromeda started a great lineage of heroes and, one day, Perseus' great grandson Hercules would be born, the greatest hero to have ever lived, so they say. No doubt you will have heard of him.

Despite his divine ancestry, Perseus was still ultimately mortal and therefore even he could not escape the curse of Chronos. Perseus died an old man surrounded by his loving family, which if you ask me, is not a bad way to go. He resides in the Fields of Elysium, an area reserved exclusively for the greatest heroes. This area of the Underworld is extravagant and beautiful; I think it has echoes of what Christians might consider 'heaven' to be like. Unsurprisingly, I am not allowed in those parts. As Hermes instructed, I was destined to reside in the Asphodel Meadows, a place of indifference for ordinary souls. This had been a remarkable gift, as those deemed 'monsters' were usually sent straight to Tartarus, the pit of eternal suffering and torment. I wonder if this had somehow been part of Perseus and Athena's deal, or whether it was Hermes' own doing? Like so many of the Gods' cryptic actions, I will never really know.

Occasionally, I have spied Perseus at a distance, wandering listlessly as so many souls do. He keeps the company of other great heroes; they seem to naturally gravitate towards each other down here. They spend their time patting each other on the back, reliving the 'glory days' and feeding their insatiable egos in a desperate attempt to still feel relevant. I like to think Perseus does not partake in this performance, but rather simply smiles and nods along politely.

Sometimes, I have seen Perseus gazing out over the Asphodel Meadows, as if he were looking for someone. I have often deliberated if perhaps he is looking for me, if he's wondering whether Athena really did keep her promise. But I have never called out to him. I am not sure why, if I'm honest. Perhaps I am just afraid our friendship won't have endured, after all this time. Perseus lived a whole life since my death, who's to say he even still thought about me? The time we shared together is so sacred to me, I cannot risk tainting it. I have so few pleasant memories to look back on.

Euryale and Stheno raised my sons, as they promised they would and, despite their eccentric methods, they were excellent mothers. Being immortal, they continue to dwell in the world of the living and they still like to spread havoc on occasion. But after my death they mostly retired from their destructive ways – perhaps motherhood softened them. I often wish they could come visit me down here, but that is a privilege only the greatest Gods can exercise. I have just had to make peace with the fact I will never see them again.

Unsurprisingly, the Gods remained much the same after my death. They never had to account for their actions, so why would they ever bother to change? You might wonder what Athena did with my head when Perseus presented it to her, in return for my access to the Underworld. I would have expected her to use it as a dart board or kicking post, but in fact she did something quite unexpected. She had Hephaestus, the blacksmith God, forge it onto a mighty shield, which would become her most famous in history. Perhaps she bore my face as a reminder of the punishment she could enforce, or maybe it was in honour of her beloved Perseus. Sometimes, I wonder if a small part of her admired the monster she had created. Did that explain my lack of punishment in the afterlife and our strange encounter after my death? Or perhaps that is all just a naïve fantasy, wishful thinking. Even after everything, do I really still crave Athena's respect? I would hope that I am above that now and yet I still catch myself thinking about these things.

And what of my sons? Well, I do not know if it was Athena honouring our agreement, or just the will of the fickle Fates, but either way I am relieved to tell you my sons both lived long and happy lives. Of course, they lived their lives never knowing their mother, but I was always there with them, watching from this world beyond.

Pegasus grew to become famed and beloved in the ancient world, admired even by the King of the Gods himself. He was known for his generosity, aiding those who needed him most. Pegasus was a symbol of all that was good and pure, ironically, the exact opposite of what his mother would be forever remembered for. When Pegasus eventually passed away, Zeus transformed him into a constellation, one of the greatest honours a God can give. Though this means I will never have the opportunity to meet my son down here in the beyond, I am still endlessly proud of him and thankful for the life he was able to live.

My other son, Chrysaor, earned himself the title 'King of Iberia'. Imagine that, the child of a cursed monster becoming a beloved king. The Fates work in mysterious ways. However, unlike his parents and brother, history would come to forget about Chrysaor and very little would ever be known of his life. I would like to keep things that way, though I will tell you that he was happy. He lived a life unobstructed by the Gods and was able to achieve that elusive gift of contentedness.

"Mother?" Chrysaor eventually found me in the Underworld, after he had passed on from the world of the living. He was an old man now, but within his aged face I saw the child I had held in my arms all that time ago.

I had endlessly longed to meet my son and yet in that moment I felt terrified. What did he think of me? Did he just see me as a monster? Did he resent me being his mother? Was he angry for me abandoning him so young? All these questions built up inside me, choking back my words. But, to my tearful relief, Chrysaor simply smiled and said, "I have been waiting to meet you for a very long time."

"You have no idea." I smiled back.

I could tell you more about our reunion, about the lifetime of memories we shared and the perfect moments we spent together. I could tell you about how it felt to hold my son in my arms again and to have him accept me for what I am and all I had done. I could tell you so many things. But I feel I have given enough of myself now and can you really deny an old soul her morsel of privacy?

Voice.

So, now you know the truth.

Perhaps you will believe me, perhaps not.

I realise that I might be doubted and I would not be the first to finally speak out only to be disbelieved. Or perhaps my words will simply be lost, drowned out by all the other narratives, disregarded for the more sensationalised versions. The reality is, the world will hear what it wants to hear. History will remember what it wants to remember.

I have come to accept that my story will continue to be retold, whether I like it or not. It is simply in our nature – sharing stories is part of what it means to be human, is it not? It is how we understand our world and ourselves. And so, my life will continue being packaged up and passed down across generations, the lies will ever mingle with the truths and the monster Medusa will remain destined to be misunderstood.

But all of this does not matter to me anymore. What matters is that my voice finally has a place amongst all the others, that the truth is finally out there. I have found a small corner of history and claimed it as my own, not as a monster or a victim, but as a survivor, a protector.

So, I have done all that I can now. I have told my story honestly and openly, just like I did with Perseus all that time ago. I have spoken out into that void, offering my voice to the world above. Now, all there is left for me to do is to stand back and wait, to see if anyone up there will actually listen.

Acknowledgements

Writing and publishing MEDUSA has been such a rewarding journey and a perfect escape from the difficult challenges of 2020. However, I could not have got through it without all the wonderful support I received along the way. And so, I just wanted to take a moment to thank some special individuals.

Firstly, I want to say thank you to the team at SilverWood for helping bring MEDUSA to life and for making self-publishing such an enjoyable experience. Also, a specific thank you to Enya, my publishing assistant, who was always on hand to answer my never-ending questions.

I want to thank my partner and chief snack-provider, Peter. Without you MEDUSA may well have stayed hidden on my laptop forever. Thank you for challenging my self-doubt and encouraging me to believe in myself. You are my rock, always.

Thank you to my wonderful and multi-talented friend, Jess. I am so grateful to you for always being willing to listen to my ramblings and ready to jump into action with whatever help I need. And also, to all my Classics girls, thank you for always sharing and encouraging my love of myths.

A huge thank you to my lovely big sister, Holly. You have always been an inspiration to me and without you I would have never even thought to study Classics in the first place! Thank you for giving insightful, thought-provoking feedback and helping shape MEDUSA for the better. I am so very grateful to have such an amazing sister.

Last, but by no means least, I want to say thank you to my mum and dad. Words cannot describe how grateful I am for all that you have done for me. Through your endless love and support you have shaped me into person I am today and without you none of this would have ever been possible. Thank you.

I also wanted to add an additional giant thank you to my mum, for reading and rereading MEDUSA more times than anyone else – your meticulous attention to detail and endless patience is nothing short of incredible.

And a final thank you to everyone who has taken the time to read MEDUSA. I hope her story helps inspire others to find their own voices and reminds us all to take the time to listen.

Having secured a First Class Honours degree in Classical Literature and Civilisation at the University of Birmingham, Rosie Hewlett has studied Greek mythology in depth and is passionate about unearthing strong female voices within the classical world. Rosie now works in the film industry where she spends her days bringing stories to life in a different way. In her free time, when she isn't writing, Rosie can be found kickboxing, finding animals to pet or drinking wine (but usually not all at the same time). *Medusa* is Rosie's debut novel, written during the UK 2020 lockdown.

CPSIA information can be obtained
at www.ICGtesting.com
Printed in the USA
LVHW100158011122
732072LV00004B/304

9 781800 420663